MY SECRET ADMIRER

Carol Ellis

SCHOLASTIC INC.
New York Toronto London Auckland Sydney

ISBN 0-590-44768-8

12 11 10 9 8 7 6 5 4 3   1 2 3 4 5/9

Printed in the U.S.A.   01

First Scholastic printing, December 1989

The voice was hypnotic.

"You're going to think I'm crazy, Jenny," the message on the answering machine said. "And I guess I am. Crazy about you, that is. Don't laugh. This isn't a joke. You're really incredible. Maybe someday I'll be able to tell you face to face. Until then, I'll just keep my eye on you. And believe me, that's one spectacular view. Bye, Jenny. For now."

As Jenny listened, she was leaning over the telephone, her finger ready to punch the save button so she wouldn't lose the message.

Who was it? Did any of the boys she'd met yesterday really have such a soft, silky voice? Or was he just putting it on? Was it a joke, in spite of what he'd said?

The tape stopped, and she set it going again. She curled up in the chair and waited, determined to catch any false note, like a muffled laugh or something, anything that would give the voice away and tell her it was a crank call.

But all she heard the second time around was the same soft message, spoken in that smooth, quiet voice with just a hint of shyness in it. That shy quality made it even more appealing.

Jenny listened to it a third time, then saved the whole tape, knowing she would listen to it again.

**Other Point paperbacks
you will enjoy:**

Prom Dress
by Lael Littke

The Lifeguard
by Richie Tankersley Cusick

Twisted
by R. L. Stine

The Baby-sitter
by R. L. Stine

Slumber Party
by Christopher Pike

Weekend
by Christopher Pike

Through the Hidden Door
by Rosemary Wells

The Tricksters
by Margaret Mahy

Ghost Host
by Marilyn Singer

Chapter 1

Jenny never knew what woke her up. One minute she was in the middle of a deep sleep and the next she was wide awake, the lightweight quilt tangled around her legs, and her heart drumming in her ears. The silence around her was as deep as her sleep had been. It couldn't have been traffic that woke her; the house was miles from the main road. Maybe it was the moonlight. With no other houses close by, they hadn't been in a hurry to put up shades, and a shaft of moonlight spread across her pillow like a milky white ribbon. Jenny was grateful for the moon tonight. Instead of spending a few panicked seconds in total darkness, trying to figure out where she was, she could see around her well enough to know that she was home.

Home. Well, not exactly. Not yet, anyway. She and her parents had moved into the house two and a half weeks before, and Jenny knew from experience that it would be much longer than that before it felt like a home. If it got the chance to, that is.

Four moves in the last six years, she thought, lying back on her pillow. No wonder she had trouble remembering where she was in the middle of the night. Living with a father whose job as a freelance consultant to shaky businesses took him all over the country and a mother whose feet started tapping after more than a year in one place was enough to make anybody lose their bearings.

A movement at the end of the bed interrupted Jenny's thoughts. Stretching her legs out, she prodded an odd-looking lump with her big toe and got a noise in return, something between a snort and a cough.

"Peaches? You awake?"

The lump moved again and heaved a deep sigh.

Jenny laughed softly and gave it another nudge. "You're awake, all right. You can't fool me."

Finally, the lump sat up. Peaches, an old dog, whose pale, sandy-pink hair was fast turning gray, heaved another sigh and blinked groggily. She'd been a roly-poly puppy and was still chubby in her old age. The closest she got to rolling these days, though, was onto her side for a snooze.

Jenny reached down and gave the dog a hug. "Come on," she said, before Peaches could collapse into sleep again, "I'm wide awake. Let's take a tour."

Taking a tour had become Jenny's solution to sleeplessness. It always happened when they moved, waking up at some strange hour, not knowing where she was, and then not being able to get back to sleep once she remembered. In two or three more weeks, she knew she'd be sleeping her usual dead-to-the-world eight hours, but until she got used to a new house, a nocturnal tour was a better way to pass the time than lying in bed staring at whatever new ceiling she happened to be under.

She slipped on a pair of worn flip-flops and made her way out of the room and down the hall to the stairs, a reluctant Peaches waddling and yawning noisily at her side. On the main floor, she turned into the kitchen, poured herself a glass of milk, and gave Peaches a dog biscuit for being such a good sport. Leaving her pet gnawing happily on the cool tile floor, Jenny took her milk and wandered into the living room.

This was the room that had sold her parents on the house, and Jenny understood why. Stretching from front to back, it took up almost half the first floor and had a soaring beamed ceiling, a stone fireplace, and at the back, a wall of windows that looked out over hills covered with pine and aspen. Beyond that, bathed in the milky moonlight, was a rocky bluff that ringed the town of Rimrock on three sides and gave it its name.

Jenny had been told that the rimrocks were a great place for hiking and learning to climb, in case you got the urge to pit yourself against the mountains that made this part of the country famous. So far, Jenny hadn't felt that urge. In fact, she hadn't even visited the rimrocks yet and wasn't sure she wanted to. If anyone asked, she'd agree that they were beautiful and awesome; privately, they gave her the creeps. She was sure they were full of snakes and coyotes, maybe even a few bears. But it wasn't just the possibility of unfriendly wildlife that bothered her about the bluff, it was the bluff itself. It was like a menacing shadow in a horror story or an evil giant in a fairy tale. It *loomed*.

It was a dark hulk now, but at the end of the day, Jenny had seen its pale, pinkish sandstone turned bloodred by the setting sun. It probably happens at sunrise, too, she thought, shivering as she peered through the tall windows.

She shivered again and then jumped when something cold touched her bare leg. Peaches, who'd ambled in hoping for another late-night treat, sat back with a guilty look on her face.

Jenny shook her head and laughed. "It's okay, Peach. I'm just jumpy. You can't help it if your nose is cold and wet. Let's go back to bed."

The dog was all for that. Bed was even better than a biscuit. It was better than the view, too, Jenny thought, giving the rimrocks one last look before she rinsed her glass and went back upstairs. Maybe that's what kept waking her up at night in this house; maybe that mass of rock that loomed over her new home had somehow worked its way into her sleep, hovering there until she woke up and faced it.

"What you really ought to do, Jen," Richard Fowler said, "is face it during the day sometime."

He stuck some bread in the toaster and poured himself a cup of coffee. Then he leaned against the counter and grinned at the look on Jenny's face. "You go over there and climb around those rocks a few times, and I guarantee that nothing'll wake you during the night. You'll be too tired to do anything but sleep."

Jenny couldn't help smiling back. She should have known her father would have an answer; he always did. It wasn't always the right answer, of course, but he never let that bother him.

"Dad, all I said was I wasn't crazy about the rimrocks. I didn't mean I had any deep, morbid fear of them that needed conquering."

"I didn't mean you did, either," he said, buttering the toast and handing it to her. "I just meant you might sleep better if you got more exercise." He fed two more pieces of bread into the toaster. "Unpacking boxes and putting things away isn't the same as getting outside and stretching your legs. In fact, we could all do with some real exercise. I think I just hit on a good idea."

Her father's voice was enthusiastic, and Jenny knew what was coming. By lunchtime, he'd have the three of them standing at the bottom of the bluff, outfitted in climbing gear, and ready to conquer the forces of nature. Her mother wouldn't mind, she knew; in fact, Grace Fowler would probably head the expedition. Jenny had inherited her mother's blonde hair and freckles and her father's brown eyes and long legs, but somehow they hadn't managed to pass on their go-get-'em, I-can-do-anything attitude to her. Her mother said she was too cautious and waffled back and forth about everything. Jenny guessed it must be annoying that their only child was so different from them, but she couldn't help it. She just approached things more slowly and thought a lot about something before she did it. Especially something like climbing that mini-Matterhorn out there.

"Richard!" Mrs. Fowler's voice bounced off the still-bare walls, and they heard her footsteps slapping rapidly down the stairs. In a couple of seconds, she bustled into the kitchen, her eyes bright with excitement. "Good news!" she announced. "I just got off the phone with the real estate agent, and we've sold the other house!"

"Great!" Mr. Fowler lifted his coffee cup in a toast. "For once we won't be carrying two mortgages."

Mrs. Fowler reached for the telephone book and started paging through it. "I just hope I can get a reservation," she muttered.

"Where are you going?" Jenny asked.

"Well, we've still got things in that house, you know," her mother reminded her. "And there might be some snags in the closing or something. Somebody should be there to make sure everything goes smoothly."

Jenny nodded. Her mother couldn't stand watching from the sidelines.

"Make two," Mr. Fowler said as his wife punched the phone number.

"Two what?"

"Reservations," he said. "I was going to fly back in a week or so anyway, to firm up that consulting deal. Might as well kill two birds with one stone."

"Good idea," Mrs. Fowler agreed. "I'll make two. *If* they have them."

Jenny cleared her throat. "Aren't you forgetting somebody?"

Her mother stopped jabbing at the phone and slapped her forehead. "Of course!" she cried. "The painters."

"What painters?" Jenny asked. "I was talking about me."

Confusion. "You?"

"Me," Jenny said. "Your daughter, remember?"

More confusion. Plus a little guilt. Had she forgotten something important about her daughter?

Jenny decided to come to the rescue. "I was talking about *my* reservation," she said. "You'd better make one for me, too. Unless you want me to stay here."

"That's it!" Mrs. Fowler jumped on Jenny's last thought. "You can deal with the painters." She raised an eyebrow, slightly exasperated. "Honestly, Jenny, of course we didn't forget you. You don't want to go."

There was no question mark in her voice. It was a flat statement. Her mother tended to do that, much to Jenny's annoyance. Assume things about what people wanted or didn't want. Unfortunately, she was often right.

She was right this time, too. Jenny really did not want to go. They'd just moved their entire household. They were barely unpacked. Just the thought of repacking even a suitcase brought on an attack of exhaustion. And if she stayed, she could arrange her room, hang some pictures, shelve some books, and generally putter around without the parental cheering section urging her to move a little faster. Or worse, organizing a hike.

On the other hand, she wasn't crazy about the idea of staying alone. True, she was a boringly responsible sixteen, and if they'd just been here a couple of months longer, she wouldn't have minded. But she wasn't used to the place yet, especially the night noises. And she didn't know anybody. School didn't start for another three weeks.

Her parents were giving each other "the look," trying to communicate without words. Actually, they were pretty good at it. And Jenny was pretty good at interpreting it. Neither one of them would insist that she stay, but they hoped she would. Her mother wanted someone here for the painters; her father wanted someone to keep an eye on the house, since the nearest neighbors were a mile and a half away. And both of them were getting impatient because she was taking so long to think about it.

Be decisive, she told herself. Be bold. "You're right," she said. "Taking a trip is the last thing I want to do. You go, and I'll stay and handle the painters."

Great relief. Her mother went back to the phone. Her father poured himself more coffee. Jenny reached down to pet Peaches, who had stationed herself under the table hoping for a handout and dozed off before she got one. "Wake up, Peach. You're going to have to be a watchdog for a couple of days."

Mr. Fowler snorted. "That dog can't watch anything, including her weight. You should take her for some long walks. Hey, take her with you when you go climbing, that'll work some of the fat off."

"It might give her a heart attack, too," Jenny pointed out. "Besides, it's dangerous to climb alone. I'll wait."

"Never mind." Her father laughed. "You're right about climbing alone, so you and the mutt just keep the home fires burning. Remember, though," he added, his eyes twinkling, "the rimrocks will still be there when we get back."

As it turned out, they couldn't get plane seats for two days, so they could have gone climbing after all. But her mother wanted to get some more things done in the house, and her father had some papers to look over, so Jenny was spared.

She wasn't spared, though, from the "getting-ready-to-go-someplace" attitude of her parents. Fortunately, she was used to it, and instead of getting sucked into their controlled frenzy of listmaking and double-checking, she offered to drive into town and pick up some supplies. Her mother, happily adrift in a sea of lists, surfaced just long enough to hand her the car keys and tell her to drive carefully, then dove back into her preparations.

Rimrock was a tiny town; people did their big shopping in Mount Harris, twenty-five miles away, where there was a mall big enough to get lost in. Even though Jenny knew plenty of rich people lived in the area, Rimrock itself didn't look it. Its trendiest store was a shop that sold candles and hand-painted greeting cards. The rest of the businesses were strictly the necessary ones — a small grocery, a veterinarian, a post office, a clothing store that dealt mostly in Levis, a drugstore, and a diner.

Jenny liked it, though. She had to admit that the bluff made a beautiful setting for a town, and since she'd never lived anywhere near a place that didn't bustle, she enjoyed the small-town quiet. Of course, it was going to be a different story in the winter, when she wouldn't be able to drive or bike into town (she'd heard alarming rumors of three-foot snows and storms that lasted for days), but right now it was warm, and the air was clear and smelled of pine.

She bought the things her mother had asked for, got some snacks and two frozen pizzas for herself, checked to see if the grocery's paperback rack had anything new, which it didn't, then headed back to her car.

She was fumbling in the pocket of her shorts for the keys when she heard the unmistakable clip-clop of horses' hooves. Then a girl's voice said, "Hi! I bet you're our new neighbor."

Jenny turned. It definitely *was* a horse, a big, shiny brown one, and the girl on it had short, curly hair to match. She was riding bareback and she didn't seem the least bit self-conscious about being on a horse in the middle of a paved street lined with cars.

"I'm Sally Rafino," she said. "I've been visiting my grandparents in Ohio, and I just got back yesterday. The first thing Mom told me was that somebody had moved into the house up the road from ours, and they had a girl who looked my age. You've just got to be the one."

"If the road's narrow and steep and doesn't have a name, then you're right." Jenny laughed and introduced herself, and after a couple of minutes, she found out that she and Sally were the same age and would both be juniors when school started.

"I thought maybe I was the only teenager around," Jenny said, after they'd chatted for a few minutes. "We've been here two weeks, and you're the first one I've even seen. I was starting to feel like an endangered species."

"Don't worry, you're not alone," Sally told her. "It's just that in the summer everyone sort of scatters. Vacations and jobs and stuff. When school starts, it'll be different. We get together all the time then."

Jenny knew about Evergreen High, of course; it was supposedly one of the best high schools in this part of the country, and her parents were constantly telling her she was lucky to be going there. Going to it was one thing, Jenny thought, *staying* at it was another. If her parents managed to stay put long enough for her to get through her junior and senior years in one place, then she didn't really care if it was an award-winning school or not.

"I guess all the kids are pretty close, huh?" she said, hoping they weren't so close that she'd feel shut out. "I mean, the whole school's only got about two hundred and fifty kids, doesn't it? You must kind of stick together."

"Yeah, most of us do." Sally tilted her head and wrinkled her up-turned nose, as if thinking of someone she'd rather not be stuck together with. "But don't worry. Everybody's pretty friendly. You'll get along fine. As long as you pass the test," she added.

Jenny stared at her.

Sally grinned. "I'm kidding. Really. Believe me," she said, "there's not enough of us for there to be an in crowd and an out crowd. There's just the crowd. Except for airheads and deadheads, of course, and I can tell you don't belong in those categories, so you're safe."

Jenny laughed, liking her.

"And," Sally went on, "tomorrow night, you'll get to see for yourself how great most of us are. If you're free, that is."

"My datebook's not exactly filled up," Jenny said, laughing again. "What's going on tomorrow night?"

"The scavenger hunt. We have it every summer, and tomorrow's the only time when almost everyone will be around," Sally said. "I would have come up to your house and invited you if I hadn't run into you here."

"Thanks, Sally, I'll definitely come," Jenny said. "It sounds like fun."

"Oh, it's great," Sally agreed. "We get one of the teachers to make up the list, and it's getting wilder every time. Last year we had to find a Mountain Lio..."

Jenny tried not to look panicked. A scavenger hunt was a game, not really a hunt, wasn't it?

"No, no," Sally said, seeing the look. "The Mountain Lions are the team from Mount Harris High. Nobody could talk one into coming over here, though, so nobody got everything on the list."

Jenny was relieved. At least she hadn't joined a bunch of rifle-toters.

"Anyway," Sally went on, patting her horse's neck, "I've got to get Emma home before she does something I'll have to clean up. Do you ride?"

"Not much," Jenny said. "I don't think I'd break my neck, though."

"Good. We have four horses," Sally said. "One of them's really gentle. We can ride over to the rimrocks some time. Take a picnic and climb around. Do you climb?"

Jenny shook her head. "Not yet."

"It's not as bad as it looks from a distance," Sally

told her. "You don't need climbing gear or anything, not for most of it. It's fun up there; you'll love it once you get used to it."

Jenny watched her ride off, smiling wryly to herself. There was no getting around it, she guessed. Sooner or later, she was going to have to climb those rimrocks.

Chapter 2

"A 'cedilla'? Would somebody please tell me *where* we're supposed to find a cedilla?"

"Never mind where it is; first we have to figure out *what* it is."

"And what about this?" somebody groaned. " 'A Countenanced Pumpkin.' That's a jack-o'-lantern, right? Who's got a jack-o'-lantern in August?"

"Who has a pumpkin?" someone asked. "And what devious mind is responsible for this list?"

Loud laughter and lots of good-natured complaining greeted the scavenger hunt list. Jenny glanced at it, but she was too busy watching everyone and trying to keep names and faces straight to pay much attention to it.

"It's gotta be Latham," someone else said. "I see his tricky hand all over it."

"Not guilty," a quiet voice said. "I tried, of course, but since Mr. Mayes refuses to use a computer, there was no way I could have any influence on this list."

"Mr. Mayes is one of the history teachers," Sally told Jenny. "And that's Dean Latham," she added, tilting her head toward the boy who'd just denied having anything to do with the list. "He's the class brain. Really into computers. I heard his room looks like an electronics lab."

At that moment, Dean Latham, a sandy-haired boy with pale blue eyes, was being teasingly pummeled by another guy who easily outweighed him by fifty pounds. His name was Brad Billings, Jenny remembered; Evergreen High's one and only football star. "The team stinks," Sally had said cheerfully. "But don't tell Brad I said so. He absolutely refuses to face reality."

Sally had already introduced Jenny around. Sally was a fount of information, telling everyone where Jenny came from, which house she lived in, how she was trying to talk her into going climbing. Even the fact that Jenny's parents were leaving town for a few days wasn't left out: Sally kept reminding people to call Jenny so she wouldn't be lonely.

Jenny didn't say much; Sally didn't give her a chance. But people seemed friendly, and she felt welcomed and glad she'd come.

Now, while the group read and joked about the list, Sally continued giving Jenny a quick character sketch of everyone gathered in the high school parking lot: Alice bordered on being an airhead, but she was genuinely nice; Marc thought he was every girl's dream of the perfect date, but Sally went out with him once and all he talked about was how he planned to make a killing in the stock market like his father; Karen was the one who'd probably make the killing; she was almost as smart as Dean.

It was obvious that Sally had everyone pegged. It was also obvious that she was something of a gossip, but there was nothing really malicious in what she said. Jenny figured that once she got to know these people, she'd form her own opinions. In the meantime, she was enjoying Sally's thumbnail sketches. It was sort of like reading the back cover of one of those fat, gothic paperbacks she'd looked at in drugstores — "Jessica, the heiress whose passionate nature matched her fiery red hair; Alexander, the dark-eyed stranger whose secret vow of revenge had hardened his heart. . . ."

"Who's that?" Jenny said suddenly as a couple drove up and got out of a slightly battered Toyota.

"Where . . . ?" Sally glanced in the direction Jenny was looking. "Oh, that's Diana Benson." Sally lowered her voice. "She just broke up with Brad. And it wasn't a friendly split, either. Brad's got this possessive thing — sometimes I think he should have lived in the fifties. And Diana's . . . well, the less said, the better. You can bet the two of them won't be partners in the hunt."

Jenny gave Diana a quick glance — very pretty, blonde, great figure — but Jenny's eyes lingered on Diana's companion. "And, uh, who's that with her?" she asked, hoping she sounded extremely casual. Talk about dark-eyed strangers. The boy walking with Diana had the darkest eyes she'd ever seen, and a lanky, long-legged build. Lanky, long-legged boys were one of Jenny's many weaknesses.

"Oh, you noticed, huh?" Sally chuckled. "I don't blame you. He's not really handsome, but there's something about him, isn't there? And he's nice, too. Kind of quiet, but nice."

"Are you going to tell me his name or not?" Jenny asked.

"David," Sally said. "David Howell. And if you're interested, which I can see by the gleam in your eyes that you are, then I'll see what I can do to get him out of Diana's clutches." With that, she took off.

"But Sally, I . . ." Jenny stopped. Sally was already with David and Diana, gesturing wildly and talking a mile a minute. Jenny wanted to drop out of sight, but even if she could have figured out a way, it was too late: Sally was already on her way back, David and Diana in tow.

"This is Jenny Fowler," she said, smiling brightly. "Jenny, meet David and Diana."

Up close, Diana wasn't just pretty; she was almost beautiful. Jenny had dressed carefully in her favorite faded jeans and a rich brown cotton sweater that she thought made her hair look blonder, but next to Diana, she felt distinctly pale and dishwatery.

A smile would have made Diana even better looking, but she wasn't smiling. She seemed annoyed at the whole world, Jenny included. "I hope you like it here in Rimrock," she said without a trace of sincerity. "You're a fool if you do, of course." Her violet eyes flicked over Jenny. "You're not a fool, are you?"

Jenny laughed a little. "I hope not."

"Mmm." Diana swung her silky hair over her shoulder. "If you're not, what are you doing here tonight?"

"Come on, Diana," David said.

Jenny didn't know what Diana's problem was, but she felt a spurt of anger. "I could ask you the same question," she said.

Diana's lovely face hardened. "I'd be careful if I were you," she said. "You're not getting off to a very good start."

Jenny tried to think of a comeback, but before she could, Diana had spun around and walked over to Dean somebody; Jenny couldn't remember his last name. The genius.

There was an embarrassed silence, which Sally finally broke. "Well," she said brightly, "it's a good thing Diana's not in charge of the welcoming committee. Listen," she went on, "I promised Brad I'd start out with him, so I'll see you two later. Bye!"

Jenny's face was flushed, she could feel the heat. She glanced at David.

"Sorry about that," he said. "Diana's not the warmest person in the world. She isn't usually that bad, though. She had something on her mind; I'm not sure what."

Jenny shook her head. "It doesn't matter."

"Sure it does," he said. "But try not to let it get

to you. You've got to be clear-headed if you're going to be my partner."

"Well, I don't . . ." Jenny hesitated. He was probably being nice because he felt sorry for her. "I mean, okay, if you don't mind."

"Why should I mind?" David asked. "The only thing I'd mind is having a fool for a partner. And the only fool around here just walked off with Dean Latham."

He laughed, and Jenny found herself laughing with him. She felt better and shoved the ugly moment with Diana to the back of her mind.

"Okay!" somebody shouted. "Let's get going! First ones to finish build the fire!"

"Fire?" Jenny asked as she and David headed for the Toyota. "What do you do, burn the lists after it's over?"

"No, but that's not a bad idea," David said. "Didn't Sally tell you? We always have a cookout at the bottom of the rimrocks when we're done. Whoever finishes first — or gives up first — gets the fire going and then we have hotdogs and stuff."

"That sounds like fun."

"It is," he agreed. Then his eyes gleamed. "But the hunt — that's the real fun."

Jenny had never been on a scavenger hunt, but she got into the swing of it fast enough. The entire town seemed prepared for them; at every house they went to, people were helpful, offering to climb to their attics or hunker into their crawl spaces to find some small item, like an attachment to play a

45 record. The clue for that had been "Platter Player. Hint: Pre-CD." Jenny had finally figured it out.

"For a girl who's been stung by the Queen Bee of Evergreen High, your mind is working amazingly well," David commented as he dropped the little piece of plastic into their bag.

Jenny didn't answer, but she didn't mind his teasing, either. He'd been doing it ever since they started, and not just about the scene with Diana. He had a wry sense of humor, and Jenny responded to it, which he seemed to enjoy. In fact he seemed to enjoy her a lot, and Jenny found herself attracted to more than just his looks.

Every time they unlocked a clue and added another item to their bag, they giggled together like little kids who'd found a prize buried at the bottom of the cereal box. Except they weren't little kids, and the prize wasn't a trinket covered with Cheerio dust. To Jenny, the prize was just being together. In between stops, as they walked from house to house or drove to another neighborhood, they talked as if they'd known each other a long time ago and were catching up on each other's lives. He learned almost everything about her family's many moves, her hopes that this would really be the last one before college, her dream of someday sinking her roots down so deep that it would take an act of Congress to get her to move again. She learned that he'd lived in Rimrock for ten years, that he thought he might like to teach someday, but he wasn't sure, that he loved climbing the bluff (Jenny decided not to hold that against him), and that a lot of his favorite things were blue: the color blue, blueberry pie, and blue jeans. She also learned that she'd never liked someone so much, so fast, as she liked David Howell.

That was how *she* felt, anyway. She wasn't positive about David's feelings, but she had a couple of clues. For one thing, even though everyone had divided into groups at the beginning of the hunt, the groups turned out to be very loose. They kept running into the others on their search, naturally, and each time, Jenny noticed that the alignments had changed. Dean and Karen and Diana were together when they'd raced toward one house to see if the owners were possibly harboring a stuffed owl. The next time she saw them, Karen and Dean were together, and Diana was with Alice and Marc. Then she saw Sally and Brad and Marc dumping a telephone book into Brad's car, and she figured that Diana had gone back to Dean. Alice, she assumed, was on her own for the moment.

"I don't get it," Jenny had commented. "If everyone keeps changing teams, who knows who won?"

"We trade off sometimes," David explained. "Somebody might have two of something, so you make a trade with somebody else to help your team."

"Why haven't we done that?"

He smiled, his eyes on the list. "We don't need to," he said. "We're doing fine on our own."

Jenny stood on tiptoe, peering over his shoulder at the list. She saw that they had ten of the twenty items. She also saw that his hands looked strong, with long, tapering fingers.

Were they doing fine on their own? She had no idea. But she did know that they were the only team that had stayed together from the beginning. If he wasn't attracted to her, she thought, he would have suggested switching by now. Wouldn't he?

David lifted his head, and Jenny felt his dark brown hair brush against her cheek. He took a step away, turned and looked at her, his lips still curving in a smile.

Jenny thought he was going to kiss her, which made her nervous. Not that she didn't want to, but she wasn't a master of the romantic moment yet. She tucked her hair behind her ear and cleared her throat.

"I think we're in luck," he said, poking a finger at the list. "Look at Number 13."

So much for the romantic moment. Well, it was too soon, anyway. She guessed.

" 'A flown coop,' " she read, " 'a.k.a.: a syndrome for parents of college freshmen.' " She looked at David. "An empty nest, right?"

He nodded. *Then* he kissed her.

"I've been wanting to do that for an hour," he said, and she felt his breath on her hair.

Jenny smiled, her face against his shoulder. "We only met an hour ago."

"I fall fast." He laughed, pulled away, and shook

out the list. "Okay, an empty nest. Like I said, we're lucky."

"I give up," Jenny said. "Why are we lucky?"

"The bluff's the best place to find an empty bird's nest," he said. "And the lucky part is — I just happen to be one of the best climbers around."

"And you're modest, too," she commented.

"I said *one* of the best, didn't I?" He put his hand on her shoulder and spun her toward the car. "Come on, let's get going."

"Let's?" Jenny didn't budge. "You might be a good climber, but the only thing I've ever climbed was a street in San Francisco," she said. "It was steep, but it was paved."

"That's okay." He put his arm around her shoulder and nudged her forward. "I won't laugh if you slip."

Jenny reluctantly got into the car. "Who said anything about slipping?" she asked as he slid into the driver's seat. "I'm talking about a major fall. The kind that breaks bones."

"That won't happen," he said, starting the car and pulling away. "I'll be right behind you."

"You mean you're going to make me go first?" Jenny kept up the joking tone, but her hands were getting clammy. Definitely not good for climbing.

"I mean I'll *let* you go first," he explained. "That way, if you do fall, you'll fall on me and I'll be the one with the broken bones."

"But that's not going to happen, right?"

"Right," he agreed with a laugh. "Don't worry, it'll be fine."

Jenny took a deep breath and surreptitiously wiped her sweaty palms on her thighs. Just think, she told herself, if you make it, you can tell Mom and Dad and maybe they won't bug you to go up with them for a while. *If* you make it. Great way to put it, Jenny.

She took another deep breath, closing her eyes for a moment. When she opened them, something had changed. The sky in the west had been filled with fluffy white clouds; they were still fluffy, but now they were crimson. "It's not my imagination, is it?" she asked. "Isn't the sun setting?"

"Yeah, but it takes a while," David said. "We'll have plenty of time. Believe me, I wouldn't climb around up there in the dark."

"Well, that's good to know," Jenny said. She wished the sun would just drop quickly out of sight instead of putting on such a long show.

They were on a straight dirt road that led to the bottom of the bluff now, and Jenny could see that it had turned a fiery red like the clouds.

"It's a beautiful sight, isn't it?" David said, pulling the car to a stop. "I've probably seen it like this thousands of times, but I don't think I'll ever get tired of it."

Jenny couldn't argue with that. The bluff really *was* beautiful. Bathed in crimson light, it soared toward the sky like some monument to a primitive god, and she suddenly thought of those flat-topped pyramids of ancient South American cultures. Then she tried to remember if those were the ones used for human sacrifices. Then she realized she'd better stop thinking like that or she'd turn into a mass of quivering nerves and buckling knees and she'd fall for sure.

"Ready?" David said.

Jenny straightened her shoulders and breathed deeply. "Ready."

The first thing she noticed was that the rocks were warm, which shouldn't have surprised her, since the sun was shining directly on them and had been all day. But she'd expected them to be cold, and somehow their heat made them less frightening. Of course, any snakes that happened to live around there might still be out, warming themselves, she remembered. And if they weren't out, then they were in the shadowed nooks and crannies, which she eyed very carefully.

The second thing she noticed was that David wasn't always below her. In fact, most of the time he was above her, stopping now and then to reach out a hand and pull her up to some minute space which he claimed was level. His hands *were* strong, and in spite of being scared, Jenny enjoyed the contact.

"I think I see something," David said suddenly as they perched next to each other on a small jutting platform of sandstone.

"How?" Jenny asked. And that's when she noticed the third thing: The light had changed again. The rocks were still warm, but she couldn't feel the sun's heat on her back anymore; the shadows had lengthened and a wind had come up. "I see something, too," she said. "It's getting dark."

"Don't worry, it won't last long."

"It won't? I always thought it lasted about twelve hours," Jenny said.

"This isn't night yet," David told her. "It's dark because of the clouds."

Sure enough, when Jenny looked behind her, she saw a mass of dark clouds rolling over the western side of the bluff. "Those are not the same cottony clouds that were here half an hour ago," she remarked. "Those clouds are definitely wicked-looking."

David laughed. "They're all bark and no bite," he assured her. "You've been in Rimrock long enough. You must have noticed the late-afternoon storms we get. A big wind, lots of dark clouds, and about three drops of rain?"

"I've noticed," she said. "But not from up here. This is a whole new perspective." She tried to smile, but her mouth wasn't up to it.

"It'll be over in about ten minutes, you'll see." David slipped his arm around her shoulder. The movement required a whole readjustment of their feet, and for once, Jenny didn't welcome his touch.

"Listen," she said. "It's time for a confession. I'm terrified. I've been terrified ever since we set foot on this amazingly beautiful rock formation, and the little storm that's brewing isn't doing anything to calm me down." She tried to stop it, but her voice kept rising until she was almost shouting. "What'll calm me down is feeling flat ground underneath my feet!"

David got the point, and to Jenny's relief, he didn't click his tongue or shake his head in disgust. His fingers tightened briefly on her shoulder. "You're right," he said. "It's stupid staying up here in a storm. We'll forget the nest. Let's get down."

Wishing wouldn't get them down, of course. Only an agonizingly slow process would do that. The hand and footholds they'd used on the way up seemed to have shifted position, or else the darkening sky made them harder to find, and Jenny spent a lot of time clinging precariously to the side of the bluff while David scrambled below her, found a secure spot, then helped her inch her way down to him.

The wind was stronger now, whipping Jenny's hair around her face and blowing grit into her eyes and mouth, but so far, the rain had held off.

"Not much farther," David said as Jenny scrunched down behind him on a narrow, sloping ditch between two massive boulders, her drawn-up knees poking him in the back.

He turned his head to say something more, and Jenny saw his shoulders tense and his mouth snap shut.

"What?" she asked.

"Thought I heard something." He listened again, his head cocked to one side.

Jenny thought she heard what he did. A gutteral rumbling, like a far-off drum-roll. "Thunder," she said. But not so far off, because it was followed in seconds by a flash of lightning.

David nodded, but kept listening for a moment. Then he gave a little shake of his head. "Stay here a sec. I'm going down a few feet. I'll be back."

Jenny managed a smile, but since he was already scooting over the edge of their little slope, he didn't see it. She pulled a piece of hair out of her mouth, wrapped her arms around her knees, and waited. The thunder kept rolling and she did her best to ignore it.

Then there was a sharp crack, followed almost immediately by a real flashbulb of lightning, and the rain hit. It was more than three drops this time. Jenny's hair was plastered to her head in seconds, and the patch of sandy dirt she'd hunkered down on quickly turned to mud.

"David?" Jenny's voice was swallowed up by another crack of thunder. She eased up onto her knees, steadying herself with one hand on the slippery rock beside her. "David!" she shouted. "David!"

The thunder was her only answer.

Chapter 3

Just wait a minute, Jenny ordered herself. David's on his way back, he just has to go slower because the rocks are wet. Don't panic.

She waited. She didn't panic, although it was very tempting. She hunkered back down and stuck her hands up the sleeves of her sweater and waited. For a minute.

When there was a pause in the thunder, she called again. "David! David, you okay?"

There was still no answer, and in the silence between thunder cracks, a gory picture formed in her mind: David, unconscious and bloody, lying on some jagged rock.

One voice told her not to be ridiculous. He knows these rocks like the back of his hand, it said. He's just waiting until the storm passes. She shook the picture away, and then another voice said, then why doesn't he answer you?

"Daa-viid!" she called, stretching his name out on a long breath. "Daa-viid!"

The thunder answered again. Jenny opened her mouth to shout, then stopped. Beneath the fading rumble of the thunder, she thought she heard a voice.

"David!" she called. "Is that you?!" She tried to block out the whistling wind and the deep-throated beginnings of another thunderclap. Every muscle tense, she listened for an answer, praying that she hadn't imagined the whole thing.

There it was! It was muffled by the noise, but it was definitely a voice. Jenny rose to her knees again and cupped her hands around her mouth. "David! I'm still here! This way!"

Just as the thunder reached its crescendo, Jenny heard an answering shout. She scrambled to her feet, ready to call again, when the lightning flashed around her like a sheet of white neon, and she heard a scream. She clapped one hand over her mouth, thinking she was the one who'd screamed, but the sound went on for a moment, then blended into the shrieking wind.

Jenny took her hand away, knowing now that she hadn't actually screamed hysterically, and shouted again. "David! I'm still here! Are you all right?! David!!"

But there was no answer. Only the wind and the rain and the thunder building again.

He was hurt, Jenny knew it. And then she *did*

scream. "David! Can you hear me?!"

If he could, he couldn't answer, and Jenny decided she had to move. She had to get down, get into town, and get help.

She scooted to the edge of her little ditch, turned around and stuck a leg out behind her, poking around with her foot and praying she'd hit something besides air. When her foot touched something solid — slippery, but solid — she could have cried with relief. Slowly, she lowered her other leg, her hands dragging in the muddy gravel, and then inched herself over and down until she could stand.

After three more maneuvers like the first, Jenny finally found herself in a place where there was enough room to turn around. Her back against a slab of dripping stone, she looked out over a wide sloping area of rocks and gullies that led to the bottom of the bluff and the low scrubby bushes that grew at its base. This time, the tears did come. Almost there, she told herself. Almost safe.

But there was still David to take care of, so Jenny wiped her muddy hands, sat down on her rear, and started scooting. Going forward felt absolutely wonderful.

The storm seemed to be fading a little; the breaks between thunderclaps were getting longer, but the rain kept coming steadily, and Jenny knew there wouldn't be any last-minute clearing of the skies like she'd seen on other days. The darkness that had closed in was there to stay, at least for the night. That would make it harder to find David, she thought. But the town of Rimrock had to have some special rescue crew; this couldn't be the first time somebody had gotten lost or hurt up here.

The picture flashed into her mind again, of David lying helpless, and she scooted faster, barely feeling the bruising bumps she was taking in the backside. After a couple of minutes, she finally reached the part of the slope where she could stand and walk.

She took a step on the rocky, gentle slope, and then stopped so suddenly she fell backward again, banging her elbow painfully.

"Jenny!" David said. "Hey, you made it down okay!"

It was definitely David, dark eyes, lanky build, and all. He was wet to the skin, like she was, and he was muddy. But he wasn't bloody. Relief flooded her, followed almost immediately by anger. In his hand, she saw that he was clutching a sopping mass of twigs and weeds. An empty bird's nest.

Jenny scrambled up, wiped her hair out of her eyes, and hollered at him. "Where *were* you?! Didn't you hear me calling? Was that stupid nest so important you left me stuck up there in the middle of a storm?"

"Wait, wait." David held up his hands. "I didn't leave you up there, at least I didn't mean to," he said. "I admit I'd gone a little farther than I'd planned, and I was just about to come back for you when the storm got really wild. It took me a while, but I made it." He gave her a curious look. "You weren't there."

"Of course I was there!" Jenny said. "Where else would I be?"

"That's what I wondered."

Jenny couldn't believe it. Did he really think she'd decided to go exploring on her own? In the middle of a storm? "You probably went to the wrong place," she said, trying to keep her voice even. "Or else you got there after I'd already left."

"Yeah, I guess. Maybe."

Maybe, nothing, Jenny thought. "Anyway, why didn't you answer me?" she went on. She wasn't hollering anymore, but her voice was still plenty loud. "I called and called, and then I thought I heard a scream." The tears were back, and she wiped at them furiously. "I was scared out of my mind. I thought you were dead! Why didn't you answer me?"

"I didn't hear you. I didn't hear anything but thunder," he said, quietly, walking over to her. Even in the dark, Jenny could see that his eyes were bright, watching her alertly. "I didn't scream. Are you sure you heard one? Maybe it was the wind. It had to be the wind."

"I already thought of that," Jenny snapped. "No, I'm not sure I heard a scream. But I'm not sure I *didn't* hear one, either." She shut her eyes and tried to bring the moment back. Yes. A shout, then a scream. Definitely. Why was David so eager to make her think it was the wind? Had he slipped and screamed in panic and was ashamed to say so? If that was it, then she'd gotten him all wrong.

David put a hand on her shoulder, but Jenny shrugged it off. She was glad he was all right, but she was too shaken up to be calm and cool. She'd spent the last half-hour being terrified, and the terror still hadn't completely faded. She took another look at the dripping bird's nest. "Well, at least you completed your mission," she remarked. "I'm sure you're happy about that."

"Jenny." David gave a helpless laugh. "I just found it, right when I was starting back for you. Come on, I know you were scared. I was, too, but it's over now. Let's go, okay?" He wiped the rain off his face and hunched his shoulders against the wind. "There's not going to be any cookout tonight, that's for sure. I'll take you home."

"Now, you're sure you know what to say to the painters?" Mrs. Fowler asked. She stopped poking around in her carry-all and glanced sharply at Jenny. "You've got the number where we're staying, in case there's any problem?"

Jenny nodded. "You left it next to every telephone in the house, remember?"

"Everything will be fine, Grace. Just fine." Mr. Fowler spoke heartily, but his eyes lingered on Jenny's face. "She's got the number, she's got the mutt, and we've got a plane to catch."

"Attention passengers," the announcer intoned. "Interstate Flight 473 is now boarding at Gate 4."

"That's us," Mr. Fowler said. He kissed Jenny on the top of her head, then picked up the two carry-on cases. "See you in a few days, sweetie."

"Bye Dad. Have fun."

Jenny's mother gave her a hug. "We'll call tonight," she said. "And you be sure to call if . . ."

"I will." Jenny managed a laugh. "Don't worry. I'll handle the painters so well they'll move us to the top of their list and give us a rock-bottom price."

Her mother looked insulted. "I meant to call if you need us," she said. "I may sound like I care more about the painters than you, but it's not true."

"Grace, we've still got the security gate to get through," Mr. Fowler interrupted.

"Go on, Mom." Jenny helped her mother hoist the canvas bag onto her shoulder and kissed her cheek. "Have a safe trip."

A couple of minutes later, Jenny watched her parents shuffle through the security gate. She waved a last good-bye, then turned and headed for the parking lot. They were okay, she thought. Sometimes they drove her crazy, but in general, they were pretty good at being parents.

As Jenny walked to the car she thought about the night before. The ride home from the rimrocks had been quiet, to say the least. Jenny was silent, still not over the scare she'd had, and David must have decided that any attempt at conversation would be futile; except for asking directions to her house, he hadn't said a word.

A long, hot bath helped soak most of the aches out of her, but the fear had lasted all night, and was still with her in the morning. Which was why her parents kept looking at her, then at each other. Jenny read their signals, as usual, and knew they were trying to figure out what was wrong.

Jenny slid into the car and started it up. It was a sunny, cloudless day, and all she had to show for her battle with nature were a couple of scratches and a bruised elbow. She turned on the radio and laughed out loud when "Don't Worry, Be Happy" came on. She decided to follow the advice.

Jenny stayed cheerful for the entire twenty-five miles back to Rimrock, but she was a born worrier, and as soon as she pulled into town, she started to fret. She fretted about the painters, who she was sure were going to be hardnosed and high-priced. She fretted about being alone in the big house at night, even though she knew that if anything bad happened, it would probably be something like a toilet backing up. Mostly, though, she fretted about David.

She had to admit, she'd treated him harshly. It wasn't his fault that a storm came up, after all. Or that she was scared of the rimrocks and that being stuck up there was like a nightmare come true. Of course, he could have tried to be a little more understanding. He could have admitted that he'd yelled and not blamed it on the wind. They might even have joked about it, instead of driving home in unfriendly silence.

The worst part was that they'd been so attracted to each other, Jenny thought. Well, *she'd* been attracted, anyway. But so had he, she was sure of it.

She was good at reading signals, and even if he hadn't kissed her, his signals would still have been very positive.

So what now? Should she just forget it, write him off as nice, but not quite right? Let him write her off as a bad sport, nice, but not worth the trouble?

Pulling into the driveway, Jenny turned off the car, but she didn't get out. Instead, she listened to the motor tick and thought for a moment. It would be easy to let him write her off. After all, even though they'd been attracted to each other, it wasn't exactly a long-term passion she was dealing with. In a few days, the memory would fade away.

But even if nothing would ever come of their mutual attraction, Jenny decided she should at least do something about the rotten impression she'd made. She'd been upset, too upset to really think about what she was saying. Now, though, she figured she owed him an apology. After that, she'd just have to see what happened. If he apologized, too, which she thought he should, then maybe they could start over.

Having decided to clear her conscience, Jenny thought she might as well get it over with as soon as possible. Howell was a common name, but Rimrock probably only had a couple. She'd find his number and call him right away.

Peaches greeted her at the door, her stumpy tail wagging. "Hi, Peach," Jenny said. "You get lonely?" She dropped her purse on the hall table and gave the dog a hug. "It's just you and me, now, Peach.

We're in charge, you know, so you have to be on your best behavior. No wild parties, okay?"

Peaches waddled into the kitchen and looked longingly at her feeding dish.

"You're too fat," Jenny said sternly. She opened the refrigerator and took out a cold chicken leg. "I'm allowed," she explained, when Peaches whined. "I'm not a blimp and besides, I didn't have any breakfast." Then she relented and put a couple of bites into the dish.

She opened the telephone book, found one Howell, and copied the number onto a piece of notepaper. She reached for the phone, then stopped. She ought to plan exactly what she was going to say, that was much better than a bunch of umm's and uh's.

Still eating, she wandered into the living room, trying to decide whether to try to be funny about it, maybe try to make him laugh, or just keep it straight and to the point.

There was a desk in the living room, a beautiful, oak rolltop that had been her great-grandfather's. It was the one piece of furniture that always went with the Fowlers on their numerous moves, and Jenny loved all its tiny drawers and cubbyholes.

She sat at the desk and rolled up its top, revealing a sleek, slate-gray telephone with a built-in answering machine, looking very out-of-place on the polished, golden wood. Sort of like a spaceship in a cornfield, Jenny thought. Then she noticed that there were three messages on the machine.

She punched the play button and leaned back in the chair to listen. Maybe David had called. Maybe he'd decided she had a good reason for yelling at him, and wanted to see her again. It would sure make things a lot easier.

The tiny tape clicked to a stop, there was a beep, and then a garbled voice saying something about the eleventh, between nine and four. There was a tremendous clanging in the background, but Jenny thought she heard the name McPherson. If she did, then it meant the painters were coming the day after tomorrow, and she should stick around the house, even though they probably wouldn't get there till three-forty-five.

There was a pause, then another beep. "Hi, it's Sally," Jenny heard. "How'd you like the hunt? Kind of wet, huh? Or did Mr. H. keep you dry?" Laughter. "Anyway, I feel terrible. I hope you didn't drown or anything. We never get rain like that here. Anyway, since there wasn't a cookout, I'm trying to get everybody together tomorrow. You know the diner in town? That's where. But I'll talk to you before then. I'll call you back. Or you call me when you get home. Bye. Wait." More laughter. "You need my number. It's 555-0071. Bye again."

Jenny smiled. Some people got tongue-tied talking to a machine, but Sally obviously wasn't one of them. She had a feeling Sally was never at a loss for words.

Another pause, another beep. Another voice. A boy's this time.

"You're going to think I'm crazy, Jenny," it said. "And I guess I am. Crazy about you, that is. Don't laugh. This isn't a joke. You're really incredible. Maybe someday I'll be able to tell you face to face. Until then, I'll just keep my eye on you. And believe me, that's one spectacular view. Bye, Jenny. For now."

As Jenny had listened, she'd slowly straightened up until she was leaning over the telephone, her finger ready to punch the save button so she wouldn't lose the message.

Who was it? Did any of the boys she'd met yesterday really have such a soft, silky voice? Or was he just putting it on? Was it a joke, in spite of what he'd said?

The tape stopped, and she set it going again, listening impatiently through McPherson and Sally. Then she curled up in the chair and waited, determined to catch any false note, like a muffled laugh or something, anything that would give the voice away and tell her it was a crank call.

But all she heard the second time around was the same soft message, spoken in that smooth, quiet voice with just a hint of shyness in it. That shy quality made it even more appealing.

Jenny listened to it a third time, then saved the whole tape and went back into the kitchen to think about it while she finished the drumstick.

It wasn't a crank call, she decided. He knew her name for one thing. For another, they weren't even listed yet, so he had to have asked information, not just picked a number out of the book. And it couldn't be a prank, a joke on the new girl in town. That was the kind of thing twelve-year-olds did. And that caller was no twelve-year-old.

Jenny smiled to herself. So someone was going to keep an eye on her, was he? It was silly, but it was flattering, too. How often did she get a message like that, after all? Never, that's how often. She'd gone on her share of dates, but for the most part they'd been extremely boring or else they'd turned into wrestling matches in the front seat of the car. And nobody'd ever said he was crazy about her.

Jenny laughed and rummaged in the refrigerator for some more chicken. The call had come at a perfect time, considering the disaster of the night before. Who cared if it was just a game? It could turn out to be fun.

Peaches ambled over, hoping for another handout, and Jenny laughed again. "Guess what, Peach? I've got a secret admirer."

Chapter 4

When the phone woke her the next morning, Jenny leaped out of bed and dashed down the hall to her parents' room. Maybe it was him, her secret admirer. All the day before she'd hung around the house, mainly because she didn't have any reason to leave, but also because she half expected *him* to call again. He hadn't, and she'd gone to bed feeling strangely disappointed.

Breathless and rumpled, she grabbed the phone and flopped down on her parents' bed. "Hello?"

"Hi, sweetie."

It was her father. Jenny stifled a yawn.

Her father chuckled. "I heard that. It's ten-thirty, you know. What'd you do, leave a few lights blazing and keep yourself awake?"

"Something like that," Jenny said, deciding not to tell him exactly how many lights. "How was your trip? I thought you'd call last night."

"Everything's okay," he said. "We tried to call

during the day a couple of times, but the line was busy."

That must have been when she was trying to reach David or Sally, Jenny thought. She hadn't gotten either of them.

"Then the O'Dell's took us out to dinner," her father went on, "and it was past one when we got back. How's everything?"

"Okay," Jenny reported. "Tell Mom the painters called. They're coming tomorrow, so wish me luck."

"Just tell 'em what we want and get an estimate. Don't argue with them, they're the only painters within a fifty-mile radius. Just a second." Jenny heard her mother's voice in the background, then her father came back on. "Your mother says don't let them intimidate you."

"I won't," Jenny said. "She thinks I'm a total pushover. I can handle them."

"Sure you can," he said. "Well, is the mutt earning her keep? Guarding the homestead?"

Peaches hadn't budged when Jenny tumbled out of the bed. "Give her a break, Dad. After all, you two gave her to me, remember? So, how long do you think you'll be there?"

"Couple of days, tops," he said. "We'll let you know when to meet us. Take care, sweetie."

"I will, Dad. Bye."

Jenny hung up the phone and headed for the shower. She'd just finished pulling on shorts and a faded blue T-shirt when the doorbell rang. Dragging a comb through her wet hair, she ran down the stairs to the front door and found Sally standing on the porch, red-cheeked and out of breath.

"I just rode my bike up here," Sally puffed. "I forgot how steep that hill is. Remind me to take Emma next time."

"Come on in," Jenny said, stepping aside. "I was just going to find something to eat. You hungry?"

"Always."

"I tried to call you back yesterday, but you weren't there."

"I know. My mother sent me on about a thousand errands. Hey!" Sally peered into the living room on the way to the kitchen. "That's a great view. Sort of makes you feel like you're all alone with nature."

"Don't remind me," Jenny said. She opened a box of Blueberry Pop Tarts and put two in the toaster. "I'm still trying to get used to how isolated this house is. The worst time is at night. It's hard getting to sleep with all the creepy noises I hear outside. And it's even worse now that my parents are gone."

"Yeah, I can tell by the shadows under your eyes," Sally said. "But I figured it was David who kept you up, not night noises."

Jenny smiled, but didn't answer. She didn't want to talk about David yet. "You want coffee?"

"Are you kidding?" Sally opened cabinets until she found juice glasses and took two out. "I'm hyper enough as it is. If I drink any coffee, I'll never stop talking, and then I'll never hear how it went with you and David."

Sally sure was persistant, Jenny thought. "Oh

. . ." she shrugged, still not wanting to talk about it. First she wanted to clear things up with David. She was saved from answering by the entrance of Peaches, who'd come downstairs to inspect the company. Sally went into raptures over the dog, who wriggled and wagged in ecstasy over all the attention. "She's a love. Kind of fat, though."

"Shh," Jenny whispered. "She's very sensitive about it."

They were just starting in on the Pop Tarts and orange juice when the phone rang. Jenny grabbed for it, but it was definitely not her admirer. "This is McPherson," a deep voice said. "Let me talk to Mrs. Fowler, please."

"She's not here," Jenny told him. "You're the painter, right?"

"Right, and who's this?"

"Jenny Fowler. Her daughter," she said. "Are you still coming tomorrow?"

"Well, yeah, I was just calling to confirm," he said. "Make sure somebody'd be there."

"Fine, well, they will," Jenny said. "I mean, I will."

"Not your folks?" he asked.

"My parents are out of town," Jenny said. "They asked me to show you what needs to be done."

He gave a low chuckle. "So, you're on your own, huh? All by your lonesome."

Jenny frowned at the phone. Was this guy for real? "You're coming tomorrow, then?" she asked coolly.

46

"Oh, yeah." Another chuckle. "See you then, Miss Fowler."

Still frowning, Jenny hung up and told Sally about the man's comments. "Just what I need," she said. "A painter who thinks he's Don Juan."

"Gee, Jenny," Sally said. "Why'd you tell him your parents were away? Don't you know you're not supposed to let people know you're alone?"

"Come on, I'm sure he's harmless." Jenny laughed, but she felt slightly uneasy. Admitting she was alone hadn't been very bright, she guessed, but she wished Sally hadn't brought it up. And why did Sally care? She'd broadcast Jenny's 'single' status to the entire group at the scavenger hunt.

"Well, never mind," Sally said breezily. "It's too late, now, anyway." She sipped her juice and smiled. "Let's get back to David. Do you like him? Does he like you?"

"Sure. I mean, I guess," Jenny said. "It's too soon to tell." She could see that wasn't going to satisfy Sally, so she held up her hand. "Let's forget David for a minute," she said. "I think he likes me, but there's somebody else who I *know* likes me. Come on." She led Sally into the living room. "Listen to this and tell me what you think," she said, turning on the message tape.

First the painters, then Sally herself, then the mystery voice. Jenny watched Sally's eyes widen in surprise, then narrow in concentration, her mouth curving into a gleeful smile. "Well?" Jenny asked, when the message was over. "I have no idea who it is. Do you?"

"Somebody with an extremely sexy voice," Sally said dreamily.

"I already know that," Jenny told her. "But who?"

"Play it again," Sally directed. When it was over, she shook her head. "It's weird. You'd think I'd be able to tell, but I can't. Somebody's doing a really good job of disguising his voice."

"Take a guess."

"David, I suppose," she said, "even though he's not the type to make a call like that. At least I don't think he is." She gave Jenny a curious smile. "I can tell you think it's impossible for it to be him. What happened with you two on the hunt, anyway? You keep avoiding the subject."

"Oh, we had an argument about something," Jenny said, still reluctant to give a blow-by-blow account. "It was dumb. But he's probably decided I'm a real pain, so I don't think he'd leave me a message like that."

Sally nodded, as if she understood, and it was Jenny's turn to smile curiously. "There's something I want to ask you," she said. "You seem to think David's terrific, and you haven't mentioned a boyfriend, so I wondered . . ."

"Do I want David?" Sally finished for her.

"To be perfectly nosy, yes," Jenny admitted.

Sally's brown eyes clouded over for a second,

then she gave a short laugh. "Well, I did, let's put it that way," she said. "But he's . . . I'm . . . oh, I don't know, it's hard to say." She sighed and twisted her hair around a finger. "He's kind of quiet and thinks a lot. Not that I don't think, but you must have noticed that I tend to run off at the mouth."

Jenny couldn't argue with that, but she decided not to say so.

"I think it really bothered David," Sally said. "The couple of times we went out, I think I drove him crazy. I thought opposites were supposed to attract, but I guess it doesn't always work out that way." She sighed again, and then gave herself a little shake. "Anyway, I'm all over that, so let's figure out who's crazy about you."

Was Sally over it? Jenny couldn't tell for sure, but she thought she'd pried enough. "Okay," she said. "Let's say for now that it's not David. Who else could it be? What's his name—the hulk—Brad? Or that guy you said was so smart?"

"Dean," Sally said. "I don't know. He doesn't seem the type, either. It's possible that he thinks you're incredible, but he'd probably send you a computer printout about it if he did." She reached down and scratched Peaches, who'd followed them into the living room. "Maybe Brad. But he usually comes right out and tells people what he thinks—he's not the most subtle guy in the world. Diana can tell you that. Of course, Diana's no gem, either, I'm sure you know. If you're interested in David, you better move fast, or she'll beat you to him."

"She's interested in him?" Jenny asked. She hadn't known that.

"She's interested in guys, period," Sally said. "For a while. And then she moves on." Her eyes darkened and her face lost its sunny look, as if the thought of Diana were like a cloud drifting across her mind. But it passed quickly. "Anyway, back to you and your mysterious caller."

Jenny was still wondering about Diana and David. Was he interested in Diana? "Forget it," she said to Sally. "I mean, probably nobody's crazy about me. This has to be a joke."

"Maybe," Sally said. "But it would have fooled me."

"Well, if he really is serious, then he'll call again," Jenny decided. "I guess I'll just have to wait and see."

"You can, but I won't." Sally drained her juice glass and headed back toward the kitchen. "I'm going to try to figure it out," she said over her shoulder. "And this afternoon's the perfect time to do it. Everybody'll be there."

"Be where?"

"Oh, right, we never did get that straight," Sally said, setting her glass in the sink. "The diner. We're all going to meet there around three for hamburgers, since the cookout was a washout. Well, I couldn't get a hold of Diana, but I'm sure she's heard about it by now. She shows up at everything, no matter how stupid she says it is. I couldn't believe the way she talked to you. You must hate her. Anyway, can you come?"

"Sure." Jenny walked with her to the front door. "But you're not going to start quizzing people about the call, are you? I really don't want the whole world to know about it."

"I'm insulted," Sally said dramatically. "I may talk a lot, but I'm not a complete blabbermouth. Trust me, Jenny."

Later in the day, Jenny got ready to go into town. Leaving on her white cotton shorts, she changed into a royal blue tanktop. David liked blue, she remembered. She studied herself in the mirror, then pulled the top off and rummaged in the drawer for something else. Wearing blue wasn't going to make any difference. She'd apologize for yelling at him and see what happened. What *should* happen would be for him to apologize, too, to say that he shouldn't have dragged her up on the rimrocks. Then they'd go on from there. She hoped it turned out that way, but if they ever did have a relationship, it would have to be based on more than his favorite color.

She put on a yellow top, then went downstairs and filled the dog dish so Peaches would have something to occupy at least three minutes of her time while she was alone. Peaches loved to ride in the car, her ears flapping in the breeze, and always put up a fuss when she got left behind, so Jenny hurried outside before the dog figured out what was happening.

As Jenny drove, she thought about the people who'd be there. Everyone, Sally had said, which would be nice, since she hadn't really gotten to know any of them. Of course, everyone included Diana, and Jenny hoped she'd be in a better mood this time. She wondered if Diana was as calculating as Sally seemed to think, or if Sally was just jealous. Probably a little of both. Maybe Sally's gossiping wasn't quite as harmless as it had seemed at first. Jenny decided she'd better not rely on anyone's opinion but her own.

The inside of the diner was as un-trendy as the rest of the town, but its red-leather booths looked comfortable and the smells coming from the kitchen made Jenny's stomach rumble. She spotted her group at a couple of pushed-together tables near the back. David was already there, she saw. And Sally, and the computer guy, Dean. Plus another girl whose name she couldn't remember. Brad wasn't there yet. Neither was Diana, Jenny noticed with a slight sense of relief. "Jenny!" Sally saw her and waved her over. She pulled out an empty chair between her and David and patted it. "You're just in time."

Jenny smiled at everyone and sat down. "Just in time for what?"

The girl sitting next to Dean — Karen, Jenny suddenly remembered — rolled her eyes. "Sally's got us playing this ridiculous game," she said. " 'Whose Voice Am I?' We shut our eyes and somebody talks in a different voice and the others try to guess who it is."

Jenny shot Sally a look, but Sally ignored it. "It's not ridiculous," Sally said. "It's fun. I'm learning a lot."

"About what?" David asked. He'd glanced at Jenny when she sat down, but he didn't seem overly thrilled to see her, she thought. They hadn't had a chance to talk yet, though. She wondered if they'd get one.

"About what lousy actors we all are," Sally said. She turned to Jenny. "We tried doing bored voices, and everybody was able to guess who was talking."

"Probably because we *weren't* acting," Karen said.

"Okay, then let's try a . . . a nasty voice," Sally suggested. "You know, the kind you'd use to put somebody down with."

Next, Jenny knew, she'd ask for a shy-but-sexy voice. Karen was right — this *was* ridiculous. If one of the boys here had made that call, he'd hardly give himself away so easily.

"I'm not sure I can do that at all, Sally," Dean said, and in spite of herself, Jenny listened carefully as he talked. "Putting someone down just doesn't come naturally to me." He said this with a straight face, but his light blue eyes sparkled just enough to show he was joking. "I yam what I yam," he said, and launched into a terrible rendition of Popeye's song.

Jenny laughed along with the others, although she noticed that they seemed surprised to be laughing at something Dean had said. He obviously wasn't the class comedian. But was he her secret admirer? His voice was soft, but slightly thin and a little on the high side.

"Give it up, Sally," David said. "I'm not sure why you have the urge to play this game, but I'm afraid it's a real dud."

"Okay, okay, I know when to quit," Sally said. "The nastiest voice isn't here yet, anyway."

Jenny was pretty sure she was talking about Diana. She couldn't see David's reaction, but Dean stared at the table as if he were embarrassed.

Sally wasn't embarrassed at all. Smiling brightly, she said, "So, Jenny, what did you think of our scavenger hunt?"

Jenny cleared her throat. "It was fun. I liked it."

Dean raised his eyes and looked at her. "How far did you get on the list before the rain came?" he asked.

"Oh . . ." Jenny glanced sideways at David. He was busy with his Coke.

"Oh, that's right," Karen said. "You and David were together, weren't you?"

"They were at the beginning," Sally said with a grin. "Who knows about the end?"

Jenny blushed, but David just smiled tightly. "The end was a washout. Right, Jenny?"

"Right," she agreed, wondering if he was playing

a word game. "I'm afraid I'm not much of a climber, not even in good weather."

"Wait. Are you saying you were on the rimrocks when the storm hit?" Sally said.

"A lot of us went up there," Dean reminded her.

"Not me," Karen said.

"Well, sure," Sally said to Dean. "I mean, there's always at least one thing on the list that you can find on the rimrocks. Brad actually insisted that we go up there to find a bird nest, but we didn't go in the middle of the thunderstorm."

"I'm sure David and Jenny didn't plan it that way," Dean told her. He looked at Jenny again. "Did you?"

"Why don't you drop it, Dean?" David said suddenly. "We got rained on, and we didn't plan it, okay?"

"Yeah, you're embarrassing them," Sally said. "Especially David. After all, he's the number one climber around here. It must be very uncool for a good climber to get caught in a storm."

"Sure." Dean leaned back in his chair and smiled. "I was just curious, but I'll drop it. Didn't mean to embarrass anyone."

There was a short silence, and then Karen asked, "What about you, Dean? Where were you when the sky opened up?"

Before Dean could answer, a waitress came to take their food orders. Jenny snuck a look at David, wondering why he'd snapped at Dean. She didn't believe he was embarrassed. Was there some kind of rivalry between these two? Dean had left on the hunt with Diana. Was David jealous about that? You don't know him, she reminded herself.

By the time they finished ordering, the tension had passed. Dean and Karen were discussing a college placement course they both were going to take, and Sally was bending David's ear about one of her horses. Jenny was trying to decide whether she should be apologizing to David or not. For some reason, he was awfully touchy about that night; maybe it would be better to just let it slide. Since everyone else was busy talking, Jenny was the first one to see Brad come in the door.

The only time she'd seen him was on the night of the hunt. A big guy, with a round face and a swaggering walk. But not swaggering now, Jenny noticed. And his round face was filled with emotion.

Sally saw him next. She started to wave, but her hand stopped in mid air. "Something's wrong," she said. "Something terrible's happened."

"Sally, don't be so drama — " Karen broke off and stared at Brad.

Moving woodenly, he made his way over to them and grabbed hold of the back of Dean's chair.

"Diana," he said, and his voice broke. He took a deep breath. "Did you hear about Diana?"

"Sit down," Dean told him. He reached across the aisle and dragged over an empty chair. Brad slumped into it and leaned his head in his hands. "They found her. Yesterday," he said.

"Found her?" Karen asked. "You sound like she's dead or something."

Brad shook his head. "In a coma."

"What happened?" Sally breathed.

Brad looked up, and Jenny saw that his green eyes were bloodshot. "A couple of climbers found her on the rimrocks. She was unconscious and her head was all — " his deep voice cracked. "She fell."

No one said anything for a moment, least of all Jenny. Her nightmare *had* come true. For Diana. As she sat there, the cool, comfortable interior of the diner faded, and she was back on the bluff, the thunder rolling and the lightning crackling around her. She saw herself yelling for David, and then she remembered the scream she thought she'd heard. She came back to reality with a jolt.

"I can't believe it!" Karen was saying. "I think I was the last one to see her. We'd been with you, Dean, remember? And then you went off to try to find a zither. And Diana — she was in a really foul mood — said she was going home."

"Yeah, well she must have changed her mind," Brad said. "When was that, Karen?"

"I don't know. About a half hour or so before the storm."

"Gee, she went up on the bluff alone?" Sally said. "What a dumb . . . never mind."

"She wasn't the only one to go up there, remember?" Dean said. He looked at David. "She must have screamed when she fell. It's amazing nobody heard her."

"I might . . ." Jenny cleared her throat. "I might have heard her."

She'd spoken softly, but no one missed it. They stared as if she'd shouted. David didn't look surprised, naturally. But she noticed that his eyes narrowed and didn't move from her face.

Brad leaned forward tensely. "What do you mean?"

"Well, I'm not sure if I'm right," Jenny said. "I mean, I . . . David and I got caught up there in the storm and — "

"Yeah, okay," Brad said impatiently. "Just tell us what you heard."

Jenny closed her eyes in concentration. "I'd just shouted for David, and then . . ."

"I thought you were together," Sally said.

"We got separated for a few minutes," David told her.

"Who cares about that?" Brad asked. "Come on, Jenny, what did you hear?"

"There was a big thunderclap," Jenny said, closing her eyes again, "but just before it came, I heard somebody yell . . ."

"Yell what?" Brad asked.

Jenny opened her eyes. "I don't . . ." she shook her head helplessly. "I can't remember." What had the voice said? She remembered almost everything else, why had the words disappeared? She shook her head again.

"Come on," Brad urged. He was across from Jenny, now he leaned forward even farther, his big hands almost touching hers. "Think, can't you? It's important!"

Jenny sat back a little. The look on his face scared her. "I'm trying," she said.

"Well try harder!" His right hand closed in a fist and his eyes glittered with anger. "How can you just forget something like that? Come on, you've got to remember!"

"Brad . . ." Sally said softly.

"What?" He swung his head toward her. "You think it doesn't matter? She could have been the last person to see . . . to hear Diana ali — " He broke off before he said it, then slapped the table with the palm of his hand.

"Take it easy, Brad," Dean said calmly. His pale eyes were sympathetic. "Remember what Jenny said. She was up there in the middle of the thunderstorm. You must have heard it. It sounded like the inside of a bowling alley." He tapped his mouth with his forefinger and glanced at Jenny before looking back to Brad. "Don't you think it's possible — even probable — that she didn't hear anyone? That it was just the wind and the thunder playing tricks with her ears?"

"That's what David thought," Jenny said, and David nodded, his eyes still watching her. But she knew it wasn't true. She *did* hear somebody yell something. At the moment, though, she wasn't going to argue about it. Brad was really agitated, and she remembered what Sally had told her, about how Diana had just broken off with him. He must be feeling guilty, she thought. He was probably so mad at her, he hoped something awful would happen. And it had.

"Yeah." Brad slumped back into his chair and wiped a hand over his face. "I guess that might be it."

Jenny knew she would remember what she'd heard; it would come back to her one of these days. But she kept that thought to herself. She didn't want to set Brad off again.

She smiled gratefully at Dean. He was the one who'd calmed Brad down and taken the spotlight off her, and she wanted him to know she appreciated it even though he was wrong about her imagining things.

Dean smiled back, which didn't surprise her. What surprised her was that he gave her a wink along with the smile. And it wasn't just a friendly one, either. She'd never been much of a sucker for winks, but if she had, Dean's slow, seductive one might have done the trick. Sally sure has him pegged wrong, she thought. He doesn't need a computer printout *or* an answering machine to get his message across.

Slightly flustered, Jenny glanced away. The others had been talking quietly of Diana; no one seemed to have noticed Dean's little eyeplay, and she was glad. The timing just wasn't right for a come-on, and besides, she wasn't interested, even though he seemed nice enough.

She took another look at David. He was awfully

quiet. Of course, she didn't blame him for that. He was worried about Diana.

But if it was Diana he was thinking about, then why did he sit so still, his eyes never leaving Jenny's face, like a cat at a mousehole?

Chapter 5

Around four, everyone but Jenny started to leave. No one had felt like hanging around any longer; after a few attempts at changing the subject, they always came back to Diana, and finally, there was nothing left to say. Diana was in a coma; they'd just have to wait and see what happened.

Jenny was going to leave, too, but then she changed her mind. She hadn't ordered anything before and there was nothing at home she wanted to eat, so she decided to get a hamburger. But she wanted to wait until everyone else had gone first. She felt slightly guilty that she had an appetite while the rest of them had barely touched their Cokes.

David left first, then the others got up and headed for the door. Jenny had just started to relax when Dean came back. Remembering his wink, she was afraid for a second that he'd decided to join her.

But he barely glanced at her. "I think I left my keys," he said, stooping to look under the table.

When he straightened up, he patted the pockets of his jeans. Jenny heard a jingling sound.

"Sounds like keys to me," she said.

He pulled a handful of coins from his pocket and held them out for her to see. "Sounds like you heard wrong."

"Okay." Jenny shrugged and smiled. "I get the point."

"What point is that?"

"That I heard wrong on the rimrocks, too."

He raised his eyebrows. "What's *your* point? That you didn't hear wrong?"

Jenny just shook her head, shrugging again. "I wasn't making any point at all," she said.

"Neither was I." Dean put the change back in his pocket. "Except that sound can fool your mind. Make it play tricks on you, make you think you heard one thing when it was really something else." He reached into the other pocket and took out his car keys. Looking at them, he smiled slightly. "Guess I didn't leave them after all. Bye, Jenny."

Jenny shook her head again as she watched him go. What an oddball. Well, he was supposed to be a genius. Maybe that explained it.

She ordered a burger and had just doused it with ketchup and taken a huge bite when a shadow fell across the table. Her mouth full, she looked up into David's dark eyes.

She swallowed as quickly as possible and wiped her mouth. "Hi," she said. "I thought you'd gone."

"I came back," he said, slightly out of breath. He

pulled out a chair and sat down, stretching his long legs under the table. "I saw you were still here so I decided to come in. I felt like talking."

Jenny nodded and waited for him to start. But he kept quiet, so she picked up her burger again. "I can't help it," she said. "I'm starving."

"You don't have to explain," he told her. "Some people eat when they're upset."

"I know, but I'm not one of them. I just eat when I'm hungry. Not that I'm not upset," she added.

He leaned his elbows on the table and cupped his chin in his hands, watching her.

"Actually I'm feeling guilty," she went on. "I mean we were up there when Diana fell. I even heard her. Of course, I was busy worrying about my own situation, but afterward — when I met up with you again — that's what's bothering me."

"What do you mean?"

"Well, if I just hadn't ripped into you," Jenny said. "I was going to apologize to you for that, by the way," she added. "Anyway, if I'd just insisted that *somebody* was up there, then maybe Diana would have been found sooner. I know she still would have been hurt, but at least . . ." Jenny heard herself running on and stopped. David still hadn't taken his eyes from her and she was beginning to feel uncomfortable. "Anyway," she said again, "that's what I was feeling."

"Guilty?"

Jenny nodded, not liking the sound of the word.

"Then you don't think Dean was right?" he asked. "You don't think you imagined that shout?"

Jenny started to say no, and then changed her mind. Was he giving her a way out of feeling guilty? Even though it wasn't true, she decided to take it. "I guess I'll never be absolutely sure," she said.

"Maybe not." David leaned back, crossed his arms over his chest, and flashed a quick smile.

Jenny was glad he'd come, but she couldn't think of anything else to say. This was hardly the time for small talk, and besides, he was the one who said he felt like talking. She decided to keep quiet for a while and give him a chance.

Another quick smile lit up David's face, and then he said, "What did you think of Diana?"

"I don't know her," Jenny reminded him with a little laugh. "I only met her that one time, before the scavenger hunt. Of course, she wasn't exactly friendly to me then, so I can't say I liked her. But like you said, she had something on her mind."

"Yeah, she did," he agreed with a frown. Jenny couldn't tell if the frown was because of Diana's bad mood, or because of his opinion of Diana. He'd never said how he felt about her. "And you didn't talk to her at all after that, while we were running around?"

"You know I didn't," she said, wondering what he was getting at. "You and I were together the whole time."

No smile this time, just a straight look that Jenny

couldn't read at all. She suddenly wished he would go. He was tense and preoccupied, and his mood was making her edgy.

As if he could read her mind, David scraped his chair back and stood up. "I'm not good company right now," he said. "I'll see you, Jenny." Then he hurried out of the diner like someone late for a crucial appointment.

Jenny stared at the remains of her burger and sighed. Why had he acted so strangely? Was it just because he was upset about Diana? Or did he secretly think she *had* heard that shout? Did he agree with her — that she'd wasted time yelling at him on the rimrocks that night, time that could have been spent helping Diana? After all, he'd asked what she thought of Diana. Did he honestly believe she might be glad the girl was lying in a coma? If he did, then he didn't know her very well. But she didn't know him, either.

After a few more minutes, Jenny paid for her meal and headed for home. She couldn't avoid seeing the rimrocks on her way — half of them turned a brilliant red again — and that didn't help her mood any. By the time she pulled up to the house, she was wishing desperately that she'd gone with her parents. What was the big deal about packing one small suitcase? And so what if they missed the painters? They could live with a salmon pink living room for a little while longer.

Jenny got out of the car and kicked a couple of small rocks to the edge of the driveway. "Stop wallowing in self-pity," she said out loud. "It's truly disgusting." It was also easier said than done, and her shoulders were still slumping as she climbed the steps to the flagstone porch. Her head was down, too, so when she went up the last step, she didn't see the basket of flowers until it brushed against her hair.

It was hanging from one of the curly pieces of wrought-iron attached to the porch pillars. They were just right for hanging flowerpots, and Jenny's mother had been talking about getting some. Now she wouldn't have to.

Jenny untangled a strand of hair and looked at the basket. It was filled to overflowing with a fantastic assortment of flowers, most of which she'd seen growing by the side of the road or in fields. Driving by them in a car, they hadn't been that impressive, but massed together in the basket, they made one of the most beautiful bouquets she'd ever seen.

She reached up and poked around in the flowers for a card, thinking it might be from the Welcome Wagon, or maybe from the real estate agent who'd sold them the house. The last agent had given them discount coupons to the local stores; Jenny thought the flowers were much nicer.

There was no card, though. And there was no pot inside the basket, which was odd. The flowers had been put in without any dirt at all, and some of them were already starting to wilt.

Strange, Jenny thought, unlocking the front

door. If I'd been much later getting home, I would have found a bunch of dead flowers waiting for me. Somebody goofed at the flower shop.

"Hi, Peach!" Jenny bent down and patted the dog, who'd come to greet her. "Did you see who brought the flowers? Did you bark real loud or did you run and hide?"

Wagging her short tail in circles, Peaches led the way into the kitchen. Jenny poured dry food into the bowl, then walked into the living room, kicking off her sandals as she went.

The answering machine was aglow again: A red number one showed that one person, at least, had tried to call. Jenny pressed the button and stood at the tall windows, frowning out at the bluff.

"Hi, Jenny. It's me again." The same soft, sexy-shy voice. "Did you see the flowers? I hope you like them. They reminded me of you, and I couldn't resist picking them." A short laugh. "I just thought — I guess couldn't resist picking you, either." There was a pause, then, almost as if he was in a hurry, the caller said, "I better go, Jenny. Bye."

She'd almost forgotten. After David's cool attitude and the awful news about Diana, and her own sense of guilt, Jenny had almost forgotten about her secret admirer.

She'd stopped frowning the minute she heard his voice, and now, with what she knew was a silly smile on her face, she hurried out to the porch and brought the basket of flowers inside. Then she rummaged around in the packing cartons that were still lined up along one wall of the kitchen until she found a tall, cut glass vase. She unrolled it from its wrapping of dishtowels, filled it with water, and put in all the flowers that hadn't completely wilted. She knew they wouldn't last long, but maybe with water they'd have a better chance of making it through the night.

Back in the living room, she set the vase in the middle of the stone mantel over the fireplace and stepped back to look at it. It looked great.

What a nice end to a rotten day. That made it twice now that he'd called and raised her spirits just when they were dragging along the ground. Was he psychic or was his timing just lucky? Jenny spun around and flopped down on the couch, still grinning. Almost immediately she hopped up and played the tape again, hoping for some clue that would let her in on the boy's identity.

It couldn't be David, or Dean. Or Brad, either, she thought. David had been so distant, and Dean wasn't the shy computer freak she'd thought he was. Nobody who could make a wink look that suggestive would bother with anonymous phone calls. And if it was Brad, then Brad had a problem. To be so angry that he'd come close to hitting her and then to turn right around and compare her to a bunch of beautiful wildflowers was an awfully twisted thing to do. Besides, she'd gotten the first call before Diana's accident. So if it was Brad, he wouldn't have kept it up. Except as some kind of nasty game. Which was pretty twisted, too, when she thought about it.

No, it had to be someone else. She couldn't remember the names of everyone she'd met at the hunt. She'd have to ask Sally. Or maybe she'd even get the chance to ask her secret admirer himself. She had to stay home all day tomorrow for the painters; if he called, she'd be ready with as many questions as it took to find out who he was.

She stretched and pulled herself up out of the soft cushions of the couch, feeling relaxed and peaceful for the first time since she'd heard about Diana. Having a secret admirer was the perfect cure for jangled nerves.

So was a shower. Checking to make sure the door was locked, Jenny went upstairs, stripped, and stood under the warm needles of water, humming and smiling to herself. By the time she got out, the sky was finally darkening. She left the lights off in her room while she toweled off and dressed, still feeling funny about not having curtains or shades, even though no Peeping Tom in his right mind would pick this house to spy on.

Wrapped in a short white terrycloth robe, Jenny trotted downstairs to check out what was on television. Their reception wasn't very good because the antenna was still lying on its side up on the roof like some broken pieces of an erector set, but maybe she'd get lucky and find a station that didn't look like it was in the middle of a desert sandstorm.

She was still turning the dial when the phone rang. Twice in one day, maybe, she thought hopefully.

"Hi, Jenny." A tired-sounding Sally.

"Hi." Jenny wasn't really disappointed. Sitting in front of a grainy-screened television wasn't an exciting way to spend an evening, and waiting for the secret admirer to call again would be like waiting for water to boil.

A sigh came over the telephone. "I just got back from the hospital," Sally reported. "A few of us went, but they wouldn't let us see her."

Jenny curled up on the couch next to Peaches. "I take it there hasn't been any change."

"No, nothing." Sally sighed again. "I thought Brad was going to punch a hole in the wall." She laughed a little. "Better the wall than your head, I guess. Did he call and apologize to you for the way he acted at the diner?"

"Uh, no. Why, did he say he was going to?"

"Not exactly. We told him he ought to," Sally said. "He came on like a real Neanderthal. You must think he's nuts."

"The thought did cross my mind," Jenny admitted. "But I guess he was just really upset."

"And feeling guilty, I'll bet," Sally added. "Diana breaks up with him and he's thinking terrible things about her, and then boom — something terrible happens to her."

"That's what I figured," Jenny said. "I'm just glad Dean managed to calm him down."

"He calmed him down at the hospital, too," Sally told her.

"Oh, he was there?"

"Yeah, and Karen. I suppose some more will go tomorrow. I might, too."

Jenny thought it was a little odd that Sally would keep watch at the hospital, considering the way she felt about Diana.

"Well," Sally went on, "I wanted to find out if you got any more anonymous, sexy calls." She laughed. "My voice game wasn't too successful."

Jenny rolled her eyes. It hadn't been too subtle, either. She started to mention the latest call, but then she suddenly noticed that Peaches had lifted her head and sniffed the air. Then the dog tumbled off the couch and moved in the direction of the front door. "Listen," Jenny said to Sally, "my parents are still out of town, you know. And I love my dog, but she's not much of a conversationalist. Why don't you come over tonight and we can . . . I don't know . . . make some popcorn and talk. Watch TV if I can get something on it." Sally might be annoying at times, but Jenny wanted company and there wasn't anyone else to ask.

"I can't," Sally said. "One of our horses has a cold and the vet's coming by to give her a shot. I've got to stick around until he comes and I have no idea when that'll be."

"Your vet makes house calls?"

"Yeah. Dr. Jacobsen is really great," Sally said. "The kind of vet who takes care of stray animals and tries to find them a home. You'll meet him probably, whenever you have to take Peaches in for her shots. Uh-oh, I gotta go," she said quickly. "My mom has to use the phone. Bye, and don't worry about being alone tonight — remember, the perverted painter doesn't come till tomorrow."

Thanks for reminding me, Jenny thought as she hung up. Maybe no company was better after all. She headed for the kitchen, thinking she might make some popcorn, and found Peaches standing by the front door, shifting from side to side.

A nature call, Jenny thought. She took the leash down from the coatrack and snapped it on the dog's collar. Once Peaches got to know the territory, Jenny wouldn't have to walk her. But she had visions of her pet wandering off and not being able to find her way back, or of being on the losing side of an argument with a raccoon, so she still didn't let her out alone.

Jenny opened the door and gave a startled gasp. Standing on the porch was Brad Billings. His green eyes were still bloodshot, but this time she could smell beer, and she knew he'd been drinking.

"Jenny," he said thickly. "I came to . . . I don't know. Apologize. Didn't mean to jump on you at the diner."

Jenny swallowed and stepped outside, pulling the dog with her. She didn't want Brad in the house.

He squinted at her. "You sure you can't remember what you heard that night?"

Jenny decided to lie rather than get into it with

him. "I've thought about it and I realized Dean was right — it was just the storm. I didn't hear anyone else at all."

He kept staring at her. She couldn't tell what he was thinking.

"Listen," she told him, "you didn't have to apologize. And you sure didn't have to come all this way to do it."

He waved his hand as if batting her words away. "I was driving around anyway. Thinking."

"Well." Jenny cleared her throat. "Thanks for coming." Now go, she thought.

But Brad stayed, his big body swaying a little. "I was thinking about Diana. She was . . . is . . ." he laughed a little, ". . . sometimes she's a real pain, you know? I mean a *real* pain, cold and mean."

Jenny kept quiet. If she didn't talk, maybe he'd leave faster.

"You know what she did to me?" Brad asked. He didn't wait for an answer. "Made me think she cared, then dropped me like I was a piece of garbage. Said she'd made a mistake." He put a hand on the wall and leaned toward Jenny. "That wasn't right!" he shouted. "You don't treat people like that!"

Jenny flinched and edged away.

"I hated her after that," he went on loudly, "but I never wanted anything like this to happen! I just wanted to . . . oh, I don't know." He took his hand away and stepped back.

Jenny waited, not sure what he was going to do,

afraid she'd set him off if she said anything.

Brad tilted his head back and took several gulps of air. When he looked at her again, he blinked, as if surprised to see her there. He ran a hand over his face and mumbled, "Sorry, Jenny." Turning around, he stepped off the porch and walked to the end of the driveway.

When she heard a car start, Jenny let her breath out. She realized as he pulled away, she shouldn't have let him drive. But he was gone so quickly. Brad's visit had shaken her and she would have gone right back inside, except that Peaches was whining again.

"Come on." Jenny gave a gentle tug on the leash and the two of them went down the front steps. It was almost completely dark, but the moonlight was strong and the cool breeze felt good on her bare legs. Peaches must have liked it, too. She stopped halfway down the walk and sniffed the air again.

A small gust of wind ruffled the dog's fur and Jenny's still-damp hair. Clouds blew across the moon and blotted out its light. Jenny heard a strange rumble; for a second she thought it was a faraway truck. Then she realized it was Peaches. The dog was growling.

Jenny listened carefully. She could hear the wind high up in the tops of the pine trees, and she thought she heard a rustle of weeds down at the edge of the road. A raccoon or a deer. Or Brad? She'd heard his car start, but maybe he hadn't gone far. Maybe he'd walked back.

Giving the leash a not-so-gentle tug this time, Jenny whirled around and ran back inside, locking the door with shaking fingers. Once unleashed, Peaches sat down in front of the closed door and stared at it.

Jenny took a deep breath, determined not to get nervous again. Brad had been drinking, she told herself. He wasn't thinking straight. He didn't mean what he said about hating Diana, and he didn't come here to scare me. He'll be embarrassed when he remembers what he said. *If* he remembers.

She went into the kitchen, got the popcorn, and poured it into the popper. She'd do what she planned — make some popcorn, try to find something on television, read a little. And forget about Brad.

As Jenny was dribbling melted butter over the popcorn, she caught a movement out of the corner of her eye. The kitchen windows were at the front of the house, and like all the others, they were still uncovered. That's where she'd seen something move.

Feeling extremely exposed, Jenny set the butter down, walked over to the doorway and turned off the light. Telling herself it was only an animal, not someone out roaming the foothills, and not Brad, she crept over to one of the windows and peered out. But it was pitch dark outside, and all she could see was the pale reflection of her white bathrobe.

Her reflection! That must have been what she'd seen before. She turned the light back on and started pouring the butter again. Sure enough, when she circled her hand above the bowl, the reflected movement caught her eye.

She finished with the butter, and then realized that something was missing — Peaches. The dog loved popcorn, but instead of coming in and begging for some, she'd stayed at her post by the door. Jenny tried to entice her with a few unbuttered pieces, but the dog didn't budge.

Her arms around the bowl of popcorn, Jenny closed her eyes and listened. Except for the sighing of the wind, everything was quiet. So why was her dog acting so strange?

Forget it, Jenny told herself. If you keep this up, pretty soon you'll be looking in every closet and then building booby traps in front of the doors. She'd done that once a few years before. After watching a grisly horror movie on television, she'd built a pyramid of soup cans topped with silverware against her bedroom door, so she'd at least be awake when the killer came to do her in. And when the pyramid had toppled, it was her mother, coming to wake her up the next morning.

Well, there wasn't going to be any horror movie tonight, she thought. And if Brad did come back, he couldn't get in.

Jenny picked up the bowl of popcorn, turned out the light, and started for the stairs. Peaches glanced at her, but didn't follow.

In the second-floor hall, Jenny rummaged in a box of books and found a copy of *Rebecca*, which she'd never read. She piled the pillows high against her headboard, set the popcorn at just the right reaching distance on her bedside table, got under the quilt, and opened the book. She could hear Peaches downstairs, still snuffling and whining at the door, and she could hear the wind rustling the tops of the trees outside, but by the time she reached the bottom of the first page, she was hooked, and soon the only sound she was aware of was the beating of her own heart.

Chapter 6

Jenny woke with a jerk, her heart no longer thumping steadily but racing with fear. She'd slipped sideways in her sleep and so had the book, and one corner of it was poking her in the cheek. She pushed herself up onto her pillows and rubbed her face. It was sweaty, and her arms ached as if she'd been clenching her fists.

What a dream! The rimrocks and the wind and Manderley and the sea had gotten all jumbled up. And Jenny had turned into Diana, not unconscious, but wide awake and clinging to a rock that kept crumbling in her hands. And all the time, she kept hearing someone shouting at her. She couldn't understand the words, but something about them terrified her.

Jenny rubbed her eyes and pushed back her hair. It was damp and tangled. *Rebecca* had been a mistake, she guessed. If she'd wanted to get Diana and the awful rimrocks out of her mind, she should have picked a joke book and saved weird, obsessed Mrs.

Danvers for another time. Daytime, not night.

She heard a shuffling sound from somewhere, and her heartbeat, which had almost returned to normal, suddenly speeded up again. The wind was still blowing outside, and something skittered across the roof of the house. Probably a twig, she thought, straining her ears for the shuffle again.

There it was. Not a shuffle, though. It was more like somebody panting, but trying to hide it by breathing through his nose. Somebody . . . Brad?

She'd kept telling herself that he hadn't meant to scare her, but what if he had? What if he'd just been acting? After all, before he'd gone on about what a rotten person Diana was, he'd asked Jenny about the shout. Had he known she was lying when she said she agreed with Dean? Had he come back again to try to force her into remembering?

Jenny shut off her reading lamp, slid out of bed, and moved soundlessly toward the door, the mood of the dream still clinging to her like a thick fog. The shuffling, or panting, kept on going, and it wasn't until she was almost at the head of the stairs that she realized what it was: a pudgy, aging dog who thought there was something outside and was doing her best to smell it through the solid wood thickness of the front door.

Jenny tightened the belt on her robe and hurried downstairs. She glanced into the kitchen; the clock over the stove said it was two-fifteen. Peaches was actually pawing at the door now. She turned her head and whined at Jenny, then went back to her hopeless task.

Jenny had often read about people going cold with fear, but what she felt was a sudden rush of heat that made her break into a sweat all over again. Something — or someone — *was* outside the house. Jenny couldn't remember Peaches ever pawing frantically at a door. Something was out there, and the dog wanted to get at it.

Jenny was so scared her heart was thudding in her ears like a bass drum. She wished it would stop. She couldn't hear anything else but it, and if she couldn't hear the enemy, whatever it was, how would she know it was about to jump on her?

Stop it, stop it, stop it! Nobody's going to jump on you, she thought. How could they? They'd have to get in first and how can they get in unless you open the door? Not even Brad's big enough to break down the door.

Immediately, Jenny took a quick mental tour of the house. The front door was locked. Back door? Yes, she remembered checking it before she went into town earlier, and she hadn't used it since. Same with the door leading in from the garage. She'd left the car in the driveway after she drove her parents to the airport; she hadn't used the garage at all. But what about the garage door itself? What if the automatic lock hadn't worked?

The thudding in her ears got louder than ever. When she took Peaches out earlier, when Brad was there, she'd left the door open. Someone could have stolen in then. It couldn't be Brad though. Or could it? After he'd left, she'd stayed out with Peaches. He could have come back. He — or someone else — could be in the house right now. Jenny spun around. All she could see were the stairs and part of the living room. Behind her, Peaches was whimpering, a high-pitched, anxious sound that made Jenny bite her lips, mainly to keep from whimpering herself. There was the basement, too, she thought. Piled with unpacked boxes, it was the perfect place to hide out.

Wait, wait, wait! Jenny turned around again. Peaches wasn't whimpering or pawing anymore, she was just sitting and staring at the door. Her ears were pricked up, but her tongue was hanging out the side of her mouth, as if she were taking a quick breather, just waiting to see what move her opponent on the other side of the door was going to make.

On the other side of the door. If someone were in the house, Peaches wouldn't be glued to the door like that. Whoever or whatever was out there, was *out there*.

They have to be, Jenny thought. And the thought made her heart slow down. She didn't feel safe, but she wasn't on the verge of panic, either. The thudding in her ears started to fade a bit, and she could hear other sounds — *normal* sounds — like the hum of the refrigerator and the dripping of water in the kitchen sink. She leaned over and patted

Peaches on the head, then went into the kitchen and tightened the faucet. She stood in the dark for several seconds, listening, and heard nothing out of the ordinary. That didn't mean much, though. Someone sneaking around outside a house in the middle of the night would try to be as quiet as possible.

Wincing at every noise she made, Jenny opened a cabinet and pulled out several cans of corn, soup, and tuna, and a couple of jars of spaghetti sauce. She opened a drawer and scooped up a handful of silverware, then put everything into a plastic grocery bag.

Peaches was still at the front door, head cocked, eyes trying to bore a hole through the wood. Jenny left her and went down the hall to the basement door, were she built a pyramid of cans and topped it with several strategically placed spoons.

Back to the bottom of the stairs where she erected another booby trap, then into the kitchen and the door that led to the garage.

She saved the front door for last. After carefully placing a fork on top of a can of vegetable soup, she pulled Peaches into her arms and scratched her between the ears. The dog was quivering with tension, and Jenny's heart started to speed up again. She tried to talk down the rising sense of panic. It doesn't have to be some*one*. It's probably some*thing*. An animal. A broken branch. In the morning, you'll find out, and then you'll laugh about it.

It was almost three o'clock. Only about three more hours, Jenny thought, and then the sun will come up, and then everything will be okay. Three hours. You can make it.

She was wringing wet, but a shower was completely out of the question. Jenny gave Peaches another pat, then went into the living room and sat on the couch. Her heart just wouldn't stop thudding, and she had to strain her ears to hear above it.

She pulled her legs up and leaned sideways, letting her head rest on one of the throw pillows, suddenly so tired her eyes were starting to close. She forced them open and stared across the room at the desk and the telephone. The red number one glowed on the machine. The message from her secret admirer — she'd saved it, of course. She was afraid to play it now, afraid to make any noise at all, but just remembering the sound of his voice calmed her for a moment.

Suddenly a piece of silverware clanged, and Jenny was on her feet, her secret admirer forgotten, her heart racing faster then ever. Her mouth was dry and her knees were actually weak. Which trap had fallen? Where had the sound come from?

Clutching a pillow, she forced herself to move across the living room and into the front hall. She'd left a light on at the top of the stairs, and its faint glow just reached the bottom of the front door. There was the tower of cans, and there, lying on the tiles, was the fork. The door was still closed, still chained. Peaches was still there, too. Sniffing the fork.

Jenny swallowed hard and felt the blood start

moving in her legs again. There was still the rest of the night to get through, but at least she knew who'd sprung this trap.

She replaced the fork, then pointed to the tower and said "no" a couple of times, using her sternest voice. The dog barely glanced at her; she was busy worrying at the door again.

After checking the other doors, and finding nothing disturbed, Jenny went back into the living room. She headed for the couch, then stopped and took the iron poker from the stand of fireplace tools. Gripping it tightly, she sat back down and waited for the night to end.

It was the poker that woke her this time, slipping from her hand and banging to the floor. Jenny's eyes flew open, then blinked at the brightness of the room. Morning, finally.

She sat for a minute, listening to the silence around her. Not a perfect silence, though. She heard a very familiar sound and turned her head to see Peaches curled up on the other end of the couch, snoring softly. Jenny didn't know when the dog had joined her. The last time she'd checked the clock, it was four-thirty, and Peaches had still been at the front door.

Well, none of the booby traps had been sprung, so whoever or whatever must still be outside. Or else they'd gone away. There was no doubt in Jenny's mind that *something* had been out there, though. And the thought of spending another night alone in the house was already starting to make her anxious.

Suddenly Peaches lifted her head and pricked her ears.

Not again, please, Jenny thought. She couldn't go through that again.

But Peaches tumbled off the couch and trotted to the front door. Just as she reached it, somebody rang the bell and then called out. Peaches wagged her rear end, toppling Jenny's soup-can tower.

Jenny's neck was stiff, her eyes felt gritty, and just remembering the night made her scalp prickle with fear. She got up, reached for the poker, and headed slowly for the door.

Then someone called out again, and Jenny recognized Sally's voice. "I heard a crash in there!" Sally said. "I hope nobody's wounded or anything."

"I'm not wounded," Jenny called back. "Just barricaded. Wait a sec." She toed some cans away, sending them rolling noisily across the tile, then unchained and unbolted the door.

Sally walked in, holding a package in her hands. It was about the size of a shoebox, wrapped in crimson paper and topped with a white silk bow. She clutched it to her chest and silently surveyed the rolling cans, scattered silverware, and Jenny's droopy, disheveled appearance.

"Wild night, huh?" she finally said.

Jenny didn't feel like joking, and not just because she was tired. She was still frightened. It *had* been a wild night, but not the way Sally meant it.

Sally poked her head into the kitchen. "Gee, another barricade in there," she said. She eyed the poker in Jenny's hand, and raised an eyebrow. "What *did* happen? Don't tell me somebody tried to break in."

"No. I don't know. I thought they might." Jenny relaxed her grip on the poker and took a shaky breath. Then she told Sally what had happened. She started to mention Brad, then changed her mind. If he hadn't been the one, then she didn't want Sally gossiping about his visit. "I should feel better now that it's morning," she said, "but I don't. Daylight doesn't seem to help. I've never been so scared in my life."

"Yeah, I can see why," Sally said. They'd moved into the living room, and she sat down on the couch. Peaches jumped up beside her and whined. "It sounds like one of those movies," she went on, scratching the dog between the ears. "You know, where the girl's all alone in the house and the next thing you know there's blood all over the place."

"Did you have to say that?" Jenny shivered. "That's all I thought about all night long. I'd like to forget it."

"Sorry." But Sally didn't look sorry at all. "Anyway, you should have called me. The vet didn't come until really late. If you'd called, at least you would have had an ear-witness for when the killer started coming for you." She held an imaginary phone to her ear. "Jenny?! Jenny, why are you screaming like that?! Answer me, Jenny!!"

Jenny stared at her. Why did Sally insist on joking? Didn't she realize how scared Jenny had been? How scared she still was, for that matter? Obviously not. She suddenly wished Sally would leave. But she looked very comfortable on the couch, with Peaches next to her. Jenny tried to shake off her annoyance and pointed to the package Sally was still holding. The dog was whining and sniffing at it. "What's that?"

"This?" Sally glanced down at the box. "Oh. It was on the porch when I got here. I don't know what it is. Why don't you open it and find out?" She lifted it away from Peaches's nose and held it out to Jenny. "Must have something tasty in it . . . ahha!" She snapped her fingers triumphantly. "You *did* have a visitor last night! Somebody who's probably very sexy, but also extremely shy? So he makes phone calls and drops off little presents in the middle of the night?"

Her secret admirer. Not once during the long, horrible night had Jenny considered that it might be him out there. But it made sense, now that she thought about it. She traced her finger along the silky bow and felt her lips curve in a smile. Well, he'd scared her half out of her mind, but maybe it was going to be worth it.

"So?" Sally got up and stood next to her. "Don't just look at it. Open it!"

Eager now, Jenny pulled off the ribbon. "I wonder what it is," she said, ripping off the red paper. "If I ever meet him, remind me to thank him. Remind me to tell him, however, not to deliver presents in the middle of the night, not unless he likes his girls terrified."

"Hurry up," Sally urged. "I haven't had any breakfast. Maybe it's chocolate, or a bunch of cookies or something."

"Why food?" Jenny used her thumbnail to slit the tape that held the lid on.

"Because of your dog," Sally explained. "She's sitting there drooling like it's got a steak in it. Maybe it *is* a steak."

"That's not very romantic," Jenny said. She slit the last piece of tape and fumbled with the lid. "But I guess it would be original. There!"

The lid was finally off. Jenny let it drop to the floor and pulled out several wads of white tissue paper. One last piece. She lifted it off. And froze.

At the bottom of the box, nestled on a bed of more white tissue paper, was a rattlesnake. A dead rattlesnake. Jenny knew it was dead, because its severed head had been placed carefully on top of its limp, lifeless body.

Chapter 7

Jenny felt her stomach churn; she screamed, a short, high-pitched scream, and flung the box across the room. It hit one of the tall windows and dropped to the floor with a soft thunk. She didn't wait to see what happened to the snake. Whirling around, she ran into the kitchen and gulped down some water, holding the glass with both shaking hands.

Sally was right behind her. The two of them stared at each other for a second, both of them looking slightly sick. Sally recovered first. She took a big breath and then let it out in a whoosh. "Talk about your unusual gifts," she said. "That has to be the grossest thing I've ever seen. Some admirer you've got."

Jenny shook her head. "It couldn't be from him. Yesterday he left me flowers." She went back into the living room and pointed at the vase on the mantel. Some of the flowers were drooping badly, but most had made it through the night. "See?" she said. "And he called, too, and he sounded just as nice as he did the first time. Nobody sends flowers and then follows it up with a dead snake. It's someone else."

"I guess you're right. Somebody must be playing a joke." Sally agreed. "But whoever it is sure has a weird sense of humor."

"Sick, you mean." Jenny shivered in disgust and risked a glance at the box. Peaches was nosing around it, sniffing loudly. "Peaches, stop it!" She said it roughly, and the dog slunk away.

"Hey, you didn't tell me he called again," Sally said, obviously trying to change the subject. "What'd he say? I take it he hasn't revealed his identity yet."

"Not yet." Jenny was still eyeing the box. Had Brad come back and left it?

Sally was looking at the box, too, and suddenly a grin broke out. "Now that I think about it, that's a great way to let somebody know how you feel about them."

"It's not! It's disgusting!" Jenny cried. "How can you laugh about it?"

"Sorry," Sally said. She stopped smiling, but her eyes were still twinkling. "I can't help it. I always laugh at the wrong time."

Jenny barely heard her. Her skin was still crawling, and she couldn't shake off the feeling that she might be sick. "Who would do that to me?" she asked. "To anyone?"

"Nobody. I mean, nobody that I know," Sally said. "Everyone I've talked to says they think you're nice, pretty, good things like that. Not that we've been gossiping or anything," she added. "But you know, when somebody new moves in, you can't help talking about them a little."

Jenny nodded. "They've said good things? Even Brad?" She took a deep breath and finally told Sally about his visit. She didn't go into detail, just told her that he'd been drinking and was still upset. "I wasn't going to say anything, but now . . . do you think he did it?"

"Brad," Sally said thoughtfully. "He does still have this idea that you heard something on the rim-rocks that night. Dean and Karen and everybody keep telling him to forget it. But he's really bull-headed. And after what he did last night, I guess he could be the one."

"But it doesn't make any sense," Jenny said. "Why would he leave me a dead snake?"

"Somebody who'd do something like that isn't making sense in the first place. And Brad's not famous for his brainpower." Sally looked curiously at Jenny. "Did you really hear something up there?"

"I thought I did." Jenny's mind flashed back to that moment on the bluff. "No, I'm *positive* I did," she said. "I keep going over it and over it. I even dreamed about it last night. But everytime I get to that part, I can hear the voice, but I can't hear what it said."

"What was the voice like?"

"I don't know." Jenny shook her head. "It was loud, shouting."

"Mad? Scared?" Sally asked. "Seems like you'd be able to tell that much."

Why was Sally pushing? Jenny wondered.

"What difference does it make?" Jenny said defensively. "Diana shouted and then she fell and screamed. It happened all at once, almost. There wasn't anything I could have done."

"No, but maybe Brad thinks there was," Sally said. "Like I said, he's obsessed about it, so maybe he decided you *could* have done something, and he sent you a chopped-up snake to let you know how he feels about you."

Jenny shuddered. She remembered Brad's strong hands reaching across the diner table toward her, and the way he'd leaned over her last night. He'd been so angry. Was he still so angry that he'd do something like this? "Do you really think it was him?"

"I think it's possible," Sally said.

"Wait!" Jenny snapped her fingers. "Maybe it's somebody in junior high. This has a real junior-high, prank-type feeling to it, don't you think?" She suddenly felt hopeful. She could deal with a junior-high prank. It was revenge she couldn't handle.

"Well, like I said, anything's possible," Sally said, "but actually, I'd put my money on Brad."

Why was she so eager to blame Brad? Jenny wondered. Weren't they friends? "I guess I'll never know for sure," she said. "But I'd rather believe it was a bad junior-high joke."

"Suit yourself."

"Speaking of bad jokes." Jenny tilted her head toward the box. "I don't suppose you want to help me get rid of it?"

"You're a great hostess, you know that?" Sally joked. "Sure, I'll take care of it. As long as it's dead, it doesn't bother me."

She went into the kitchen and came back with a handful of paper towels. Turning the box over, she gingerly used the towels to scoop the two pieces of snake back into it. "There," she said, fitting the lid back on. "Out of sight, out of mind, right? I have to go, so I'll put it in that big garbage can next to the garage."

"Wait." Sally was already heading for the front door and Jenny followed her. "You never said why you came in the first place."

"I knew I forgot something!" Sally said. "I came because my mother was on one of her marathon calls, so I couldn't use the phone, and I wanted to see if you'd like to go horseback riding."

"Now?"

"Well, you probably ought to change first," Sally suggested, looking pointedly at Jenny's robe. "But yes, soon. I've only got about an hour or so and then I have to do about a thousand other things."

"I'd love to go," Jenny said. Right now, she'd do anything to get out of the house. Then she heard the unmistakable sound of a truck pulling into the driveway. She peered out the front door, then turned back to Sally. "But I can't. The painters are here."

Sally looked out at the truck and grinned. "Well, just offer them coffee and fried rattlesnake. That'll get rid of them fast!" she said as she was leaving.

Jenny didn't mention the snake, but she did offer McPherson and Son coffee, expecting them to refuse. They accepted. They followed her into the kitchen and seated themselves at the table as if this were the usual way of doing business. McPherson the elder blew on his coffee and settled back in the chair. "So, young lady. Who do we talk to?"

"Talk to? Oh," Jenny said, realizing he expected to deal with her parents. "Me. I'll show you what we want done and you can give me a price."

McPherson the younger was about thirty, Jenny thought, and she noticed that he hadn't taken his eyes off her bathrobe since he'd come in the house. "You're still alone here, then?" he asked.

"Yes." Jenny cleared her throat. "For the moment," she added. The guy made her nervous. Why had she bothered with the coffee? "Look, I'm expecting someone in just a few more minutes. Why don't you bring your cups with you and I'll show you the rooms."

Without waiting for an answer, Jenny strode into the entry hall. "This," she said, gesturing at the walls. She turned and went into the living room. "And this." Turning again, she went back to the entrance and pointed up the stairs. "And the hallway up there."

The two of them started up the stairs. Halfway

up, the younger man glanced down at her and smiled. "You're not coming?"

Jenny shook her head and stayed by the front door.

"Oh, right, you're expecting company." He smiled again, as if he were on to her lie, and followed his father up the stairs.

Jenny waited, wishing somebody *would* come. A friendly face would be very welcome right about now.

The McPhersons were back in a couple of minutes. The elder gave her the price and Jenny nodded. "That sounds fine," she said, even though it seemed outrageously high. "I'll tell my parents and let you know tomorrow."

"Don't wait too long," the younger man told her, letting his eyes drift over her bathrobe again. "We can slot you in in ten days, but after that, who knows?"

"I'll just have to take my chances," Jenny said. She pulled the door open wide and stepped back to let them through. "Thanks for coming."

"Oh, it was our pleasure," he said.

Jenny shut the door behind them and leaned against it for a second. Then she raced upstairs and into the shower. It felt so good to finally be taking one that she didn't even think about the snake until she was blowing her hair dry. She shuddered, but her stomach stayed steady.

Back downstairs and dressed at last, Jenny took Peaches outside, then brought her in and gave her some unbuttered popcorn as a peace offering for yelling at her. She deserved it. After all, she'd heard something and kept watch almost the entire night.

"Wait till Dad hears about it, Peach," Jenny said, patting her as she wolfed down the popcorn. "He won't be making any more cracks about what a fat, lazy good-for-nothing you are. And if he does, we'll just remind him of The Night You Smelled the Snake."

Jenny's stomach churned again, but not from the memory of her surprise package. While she filled the dog dish with kibble, she thought about what she'd eaten in the last sixteen hours: no dinner to speak of and no breakfast at all. It was past noon now, so no wonder her stomach was acting up. She was famished.

Well, there was plenty of soup and canned vegetables, she thought wryly. Also a couple of frozen pizzas, guaranteed to taste like oregano-sprinkled cardboard. And there was peanut butter. She didn't want any of it, so she decided to go into town and buy something she did want.

It felt good to be out of the house and driving. She turned up the radio and cranked down the window, enjoying the feel of the wind in her hair. There was never any traffic on this road, and her mind drifted. She refused to think about the snake, or Brad, or anything unpleasant. Instead, she thought about what kind of food she'd buy and whether she should get her hair cut chin-length. And she thought about her secret admirer. She was halfway into

Rimrock before she noticed the car behind her.

A blue Toyota, a little worse for wear, and very familiar. It was David's car; Jenny recognized it the minute she turned onto the main street. Had he been following her or was this just a coincidence?

Finding a parking place was no problem, as usual. She had her pick and pulled into one right in front of the grocery store. The Toyota pulled in next to her. Jenny got out and so did David. Tall, loose-limbed, dark-eyed David.

"I tried to call you a little while ago," he said, joining her on the sidewalk.

No "Hi, how's it going?" she noticed. No small talk. "I guess I was . . . ?" Where? She hadn't left the house since late yesterday afternoon. "Oh. In the shower. But we have a machine." Except there hadn't been any new message on it when she left.

"I know. I didn't use it. I hate those things."

Loose-limbed, dark-eyed, old-fashioned David, she thought. "Well. So. Why did you call?" No beating around the bush for her, either.

He stuck his hand into the pocket of his jeans and pulled something out. A bracelet, woven of narrow, multi-colored strands of cloth. "I found this in my car this morning," he said, holding it out to her. "I guess it fell off some time that night."

No need to ask *what* night. Jenny remembered now that she'd worn it, but she hadn't missed it at all. "Well. Thanks." She slipped it over her hand and smiled at him. She'd been complimented on her smile a few times in her life; supposedly it brought out a dimple at the corner of her mouth, although she'd never been able to see it. According to her mother, it also lit up her face and made people want to smile back. Jenny always thought her mother was just prejudiced, and now she was sure of it, because David wasn't smiling back at all. She cleared her throat. "Have you . . . um . . . been to see Diana?"

"I've been to the hospital," he said. "But nobody can see her except her family."

"Is she still the same?"

He nodded.

"That's too bad." That sounded awfully weak, but Jenny couldn't think of anything else.

However, David didn't seem to be listening to her lame conversation. He was looking at her again the way he had in the diner, as if she were fascinating but frightening.

Jenny stood it as long as she could and then laughed nervously. "Is there something stuck on my teeth?" she finally asked. "If there is, please tell me and I'll get rid of it."

This time he did smile, and little pinpoints of light flashed in his nearly black eyes as they took in her cutoffs and faded blue workshirt. "No, you look great, Jenny."

"Well, that's good. The way you were staring at me, I felt like I was under a microscope."

"Sorry," he said, running a hand through his hair. "I've been thinking."

Jenny waited.

David looked at the sky, as if he were inspecting it for signs of rain. The sky was clear. Finally he said, "About that night."

Back to that, Jenny thought. She guessed she couldn't blame him, but she really didn't want to talk about it.

"You remember, when I found you . . . or you found me, or whatever, you said you'd heard a scream? And then, at the diner," he went on, "you said it again. Brad was all over you about it and you changed your mind and said it was the wind. You said that when I came back, too. When you were eating."

"I didn't exactly say that," Jenny reminded him. "I said I'd probably never know. And before, when Dean said it must have been the storm, I went along with it because I didn't feel like getting punched or strangled."

"Okay, good."

"Good?"

"Yeah, you didn't change your mind, you just backed off." David's eyes were slits now and his voice was quiet and intense. Jenny felt like she was under a hot spotlight.

"What's good about it?" she asked.

"It means you *did* hear something," he said. "And I want to know what it was. It's like trying to put a puzzle together, you know? Only a piece is missing. And you've got it."

"*You're* the puzzle, David," Jenny gave another nervous laugh. He was so edgy he almost scared her. "I mean, okay, so I heard a scream or a shout or something. But I can't remember what it was. I've tried, but I just can't." She fiddled with the cloth bracelet, twisting it around her wrist. "And . . . this is going to sound really heartless, I know, and I don't mean it to — but what difference does it make what I heard?"

"It's . . ." he shook his head impatiently. "Look, I can't get into it. But it could make a lot of difference."

Suddenly he reached out with both hands, as if he were going to take her by the shoulders and shake her. He didn't do it, but Jenny could tell he still wanted to.

"I don't see why," she said. She was uncomfortable, but her nervousness was fading and she was starting to get annoyed. "She probably yelled 'help' or 'oh, no,' or something like that. Whatever it was, she said it right before she fell, and there was nothing anybody could do, unless maybe they'd been standing next to her."

"That's what I'm . . ." Another quick shake of the head. "You don't understand, Jenny."

"Well, explain it to me, then! I'm not dense."

"I can't!" This time David did grab her shoulders. "I just wish you'd try to remember. It's important!"

She shook herself free and stepped back. "First Brad and now you," she said. "I'm sorry I ever mentioned it in the first place, and I'm sick of feeling guilty about something that wasn't my fault!"

"That isn't — "

"Look, let's just forget it," she interrupted. "I don't want to talk about it." She turned to leave and then spun around. "I heard something, but I can't remember what it was, and I'm not going to try anymore! I wish I'd never been up there in the first place!"

Jenny spun back toward her car, just in time to see a group of kids coming down the sidewalk toward them. Karen and Dean and a girl she didn't recognize. She'd been shouting at the end, and she could tell by the looks on their faces that they'd heard what she'd said, but she marched back to her car without a word, her face blazing hot. Let David be the one to explain why she'd been shrieking at him on the street.

If the main street of Rimrock hadn't been paved, she would have roared off in a cloud of dust, but she had to be satisfied with just gunning the motor before she pulled away. She didn't want to give him the satisfaction of looking back, but she did glance discreetly in the rearview mirror. There he was, hands stuffed in his pockets, talking to the others.

Probably telling them a complete lie, she thought. Oh, he was tricky. All that cute, little-boy stuff he'd pulled at first — looking at the sky, running his hand through his hair — he'd done everything but scuff the toe of his sneaker in the dirt. And all the time he was just working up to making her feel guilty about Diana. He'd conveniently forgotten, of course, that when they'd met up on the rimrocks that night, *he* was the one who suggested that the storm had played tricks with her hearing. And now that they knew what had happened to Diana, he wanted Jenny to remember, so he could wallow in a bunch of "If only's."

Well, too bad. She wasn't going to accommodate him. She was through trying to remember what she'd heard, and she was going to do her best to bury that night at the bottom of her memory pile.

Jenny's anger carried her most of the way home. It wasn't until she was on the long, empty stretch of road that led to her turnoff that she calmed down enough to notice how fast she was driving. She eased up on the gas pedal, even though she knew it wouldn't matter. Not once on this road had she ever seen a police car. In fact, the first time she'd encountered any car was earlier, when she'd seen David's Toyota behind her.

Not quite furious anymore, but still plenty mad, Jenny sped up the hill to her house and all but stomped inside. Peaches was waiting, as usual, looking as if she'd just waked up.

She gave the dog an absent-minded pat, walked into the living room, and was all set to fling herself onto the couch when she noticed that the answering machine had a message on it.

If she ever needed an admiring phone call, this would be the time. She punched the button eagerly, crossing her fingers and wondering what he'd say. Would he finally reveal who he was, or was he going to keep the tantalizing game going a little longer?

Chapter 8

But instead of the soft, enticing voice of her secret admirer, Jenny heard her father's voice boom out: "Jen! Looks like we'll be a few days longer than we thought. The house deal hit a couple of snags, nothing that can't be worked out, although your mother is ready to throttle everybody in sight. As soon as we know when we're coming back, we'll give you the word. Call and tell us how you're doing, but not tonight. We'll be out. Hope the mutt's earning her keep."

Oddly enough, the first thing that occurred to Jenny was not that she'd have to spend two, maybe three more nights alone in the house. Her first thought was the painters. She'd promised to call them tomorrow. *Then* she thought about being alone in the house and a shiver ran through her.

"First things first," she said out loud. She checked the number where her parents were staying and dialed it.

"Mom, hi, I just got Dad's message."

"And you've called to offer your condolences, I hope." Mrs. Fowler sounded harried, to say the least. "These people! They actually want us to include that gorgeous lighting fixture in the asking price!"

"What gorgeous lighting fixture?"

"The one in the dining room. The one from Italy?" Jenny's mother made it sound as if she'd made a special trip to Italy just to buy it, when she'd actually found it at a neighborhood garage sale. It wasn't gorgeous, either, not in Jenny's opinion. It was kind of hideous, now that she thought about it — lots of fat globes that needed dusting all the time.

"Well, I'm sure you'll work it out," Jenny said.

"You sound like your father," Mrs. Fowler sighed. "The lamp isn't the only thing they want, you know."

"Okay, well then, call off the deal," Jenny suggested.

Her mother gasped. "Do you realize what that would mean?" she asked. "The real estate market isn't exactly booming here; if we don't sell it now, we'll . . ."

"Mom!" Jenny broke in. "I didn't call about the house. I called about the painters."

That got Mrs. Fowler's attention. "All right," she said, as if expecting the worst. "Let me have it."

"It's highway robbery," she announced when Jenny had finished. "But tell them we agree. Of course, if this house deal falls through, we'll just have to live with salmon walls for the next twenty years."

Jenny swallowed a laugh and decided not to mention that they could do the painting themselves. Which would be a lot better than having that creep McPherson in the house. But her mother obviously wasn't in the mood for solutions. She was enjoying the problems too much.

"Well." Mrs. Fowler sighed again. "Anything else?"

"That's all," Jenny said. No need to mention headless snakes and sleepless nights. Her mother would pooh-pooh the whole thing as the product of somebody's small mind, not worthy of worry. And she'd be right, Jenny told herself firmly. "Just let me know when you'll be coming back so I can meet you."

"Oh, we will. If we ever do get back." On that optimistic note, her mother said she had to go. Back to the battle, Jenny supposed.

As soon as she hung up, the thought of the empty house leaped into her mind, but she pushed it away. Busy, she decided. She'd keep so busy she wouldn't have time to get scared.

First she called McPherson & Son, left word on their answering machine that the Fowlers of Rimrock would be ready to have them start painting as soon as possible, and asked them to call back and tell her the exact date.

Next she called Sally. "Another ten seconds and you'd have missed me," Sally said. "I was just on my way out the door. What's up? Don't tell me you got another charming present."

"No, and please don't mention it again," Jenny told her. "I'm trying to erase it from my memory. I'm also trying to pretend that being alone here is perfectly wonderful."

"And it's not?"

"Well, so far it's okay, but that's because it isn't dark yet," Jenny said. "When the sun goes down, I just might turn into a blubbering idiot, so I thought I'd see if you wanted to come spend the night." Sally wasn't perfect, but Jenny couldn't be picky. "We could listen to music, and I think I can figure out how to hook up the VCR, so we could watch a tape. All you'd have to bring is yourself. And some food," she added, suddenly remembering that she never did make it to the grocery store. "Unless you'd be satisfied with frozen pizza and peanut butter."

"Sorry," Sally said.

"I don't blame you," Jenny said. "Maybe you could buy some stuff and then come over. I'd pay you back."

"No, I mean I'm sorry I can't come," Sally told her. "I wish I could, believe me. Some friends of my parents are having a cookout. They do it every summer and it's extremely boring. But since they live fifty miles away and we hardly ever see them, I have to go. We won't be getting back until really late. Sorry," she said again.

"Oh, that's okay." Jenny tried to sound unconcerned. "It's dumb for me to be scared, anyway. Nothing's going to happen."

"Right," Sally agreed. "Brad or whoever wouldn't play another prank so soon after the first one. They'll wait awhile until they're sure you've forgotten all about it. *Then* they'll spring the second one on you."

"Thanks a lot."

"Whoops — forget I said that. Listen," Sally went on. "I can't help you out tonight, but how about tomorrow morning?"

"Assuming I'm still alive?" Jenny asked. Maybe joking about it would help.

"Come on," Sally said. "Just lock all the doors and leave all the lights on. Anyway, why don't we go riding in the morning? Early, like for breakfast? I'll supply the horses and the food and we'll ride to the bottom of the bluff and build a fire and fry bacon and eggs."

Jenny didn't have to think about it twice. "I'll be ready," she said. "And we can go as early as you want, since I just might stay awake all night."

"Then you'd better ride Alice," Sally said. "She's practically geriatric, so you'll be able to take a nap on the way."

They finished making their plans, and when Jenny hung up, she realized she was ravenous. The thought of tomorrow's bacon and eggs made her stomach rumble wildly, and she wished she had some now. If it hadn't been for meeting David, she probably would.

An image flashed into her mind: David standing close to her on the sidewalk, the lights in his eyes like two piercing spotlights as his strong hands reached for her. And she saw in the image something she hadn't noticed at the time it was happening. He was anxious and upset, yes, but he was also . . . what? Scared? Desperate? She couldn't give a name to the emotion she saw in his eyes, and that bothered her. Maybe if she hadn't lashed out at him, if she'd given him a chance to explain, then their meeting might have ended in a different way.

Her glance strayed to the telephone, but as it did, the image of David changed. The confusing emotion in his eyes faded; all she saw was the anger, and she felt his fingers digging hard into her shoulders again.

Of course he wasn't scared, she thought. She'd only been imagining it. And he hadn't seemed about to offer any explanations.

She blinked, and David's image faded completely. The only vision in her mind now was a table spread with food. Peaches at her heels, she went into the kitchen and unearthed two cans of chili and a box of instant rice. Ten minutes later, she poured the chili over the rice and dug in. Nothing had ever tasted so good, and she'd made so much there'd be enough for later that night, when she was sure to be hungry again.

But if Jenny's stomach rumbled for more food later that night, she didn't hear it. After shelving books for a few hours, something she'd been planning to do ever since her parents left, she hooked up the VCR, put on a movie — an inane comedy, with absolutely no hint of scariness to it — and stretched out on the couch to watch it. She might have seen ten minutes of it, but that was all. Her eyelids drooped, and she forced them open a few times, but then they closed for good. When she woke, it was just past seven in the morning.

By eight-thirty, she and Sally were astride Emma and Alice, plodding their way slowly toward the base of the rimrocks. The sun wasn't up very high yet. It would get hot later on, but right now the air was cool and fresh.

Jenny smiled to herself. It was amazing what eleven hours of sleep could do for a person, she thought. Eleven hours of sleep made it easy to believe that nothing weird, like a dead snake arriving in a giftbox, would ever happen again. Sleep made it hard to believe it really *had* happened. It made Brad seem pathetic, and turned the argument with David into a bad but fading memory. Even the thought of spending a couple of more nights alone in the house wasn't as terrible.

Mostly, eleven hours of sleep and not enough food made her wish Alice wasn't quite as slow as Sally had promised. "Hey, I'm starving!" she called out. "I think I can manage not to fall off if we speed up the pace a little!"

"Okay, then just give her a tap with your heels," Sally instructed. "And don't forget to hang on."

"To what?" Jenny asked. They were riding bareback.

"To her mane," Sally said. "Or wrap your arms around her neck."

One tap of Jenny's heels put Alice into a jaw-rattling trot, and Jenny had to clutch her mane tightly or she would have ended up on the ground. But with a second tap, Alice broke into an easy, rocking-horse lope. It felt wonderful, and Jenny was almost sorry when they had to slow down so the horses could pick their way around the rocks at the bottom of the bluff.

"That was fantastic," she said as she slid to the ground. "Let's do it again. Like tomorrow, maybe."

"I can't tomorrow." Sally took the knapsack off her back and ran her fingers through her curly hair. "I won't be here tomorrow."

"Oh? Where are you going?"

"My aunt's," Sally said shortly. "She's a pain. Come on, let's get going."

For once, Sally didn't seem talkative. "So you're leaving in the morning?" Jenny asked.

"Late this afternoon." Sally hoisted the knapsack to her shoulder again. "Come on, let's find a good spot to eat."

Jenny looked uncertainly at the horses.

"Don't worry," Sally told her, sounding annoyed. "They won't wander, and anyway, we're not climbing far. Pick up some dry twigs on the way; we'll need them for the fire." With that, she was gone, urging Jenny to hurry up.

Sally knew her way around the rimrocks as well as David, Jenny noticed, as she watched her scramble nimbly up the side of what looked like a completely smooth boulder. Jenny found a gully beside it and used that instead. "You'll never learn to climb that way," Sally said. "And it's taking you forever."

"What's the rush?" Jenny asked, slowly pulling herself up beside Sally.

"Nothing, never mind." Sally set the knapsack down. "We're here."

Jenny stood up and looked around. The rock they were on was very wide and almost flat on top, except for some little basin-type indentations that would be perfect for a fire. The sun was higher up now, but there was a huge outcropping of rocks several feet above that gave them shade and still left them room to stand. Jenny walked gingerly to the edge of their rock and looked over. They hadn't climbed high enough for her to see the town, but she could see Emma and Alice, not very far below, still munching the apples Sally had brought for them.

Jenny took a deep breath. She thought she'd hate being up here again, but they were on the opposite side from where she and David had been. Besides, it was beautiful in the morning. It would be a perfect place for a date. A breakfast date, she thought. David's lean, handsome face came to mind immediately, and she thought again about calling him. She'd decided this morning not to. Sure, she'd lost her temper, but he was the one who'd started the whole thing by acting so strangely. Let him do the calling. Now, though, she was starting to lean the other way. She sighed and shook her head, wishing she could for once make up her mind and have it stay made up.

She heard a sound behind her and turned. Sally had gathered the twigs together and was setting a match to them. Her hair was falling in her face, and she had her tongue clamped between her teeth in concentration. Jenny hadn't mentioned the sidewalk encounter with David. Should she tell Sally? Of course, Sally probably knew already. She seemed to know everything that went on. But if she knew, she probably would have brought it up by now. She wasn't the type to hold back out of politeness. But Sally seemed edgy this morning. She seemed to have something on her mind. Jenny wondered what it was and realized that she didn't know her all that well. She usually talked a lot, but not about feelings or things like that. Maybe she was just what she seemed to be — frank and friendly, with no murky, hidden feelings at all.

"Hey."

Jenny turned and saw that Sally had the fire going and was digging into the knapsack for the food. She tossed Jenny the packet of bacon. "Open that, why don't you?"

Jenny tackled the bacon, glad she'd decided not to talk about David. She was beginning to wish she hadn't come, and wondered why Sally had bothered, since she was in such a bad mood.

Sally hadn't brought eggs; there was only one

left in her refrigerator. But she'd brought a loaf of Italian bread and a chunk of cheddar cheese, and when the bacon was done, they made enough sandwiches for six people. Jenny ate hungrily, but Sally just picked at the food.

"I'm so stuffed I can't move," Jenny said when she'd finished. "I may just have to stay up here all day."

"I do sometimes," Sally said. "Or I stay for hours, anyway. I love it up here." She was standing at the edge of the rock, keeping an eye on the horses. She checked her watch, then said, "Come on over here. The view's great."

Jenny scooted over and sat next to her. "I can see why you love it. Now," she added, "the other night, I hated it."

"Well, nobody in their right mind would like it in a storm," Sally said. "A couple of kids say they're afraid of it after what it did to Diana."

"I take it you're not one of them."

"Do I look afraid?" Sally asked.

Jenny started to say that she looked worried, but she changed her mind. If Sally wanted to talk, she would. "How is Diana?" she asked.

"The same." Sally checked the time again, then shoved her hands in the back pockets of her jeans.

"Do you want to go or something?" Jenny asked. Sally flushed. "Why?"

"Well, you keep looking at your watch," Jenny said. "If you've got to leave, then just say so."

"It's my aunt," Sally said quickly. "I keep checking the time because I keep hoping it's magically slowed down. My aunt's a pain. I don't want to go visit her."

"I guess everybody has at least one relative like that." Jenny lay back on the rock and squinted up at the sky. She was just about to say more when she heard a faint, swishing sound, and suddenly her face was covered with dust and grit. "Where'd that come from?" She reached up to brush it off.

"What?" Sally was still gazing at the horses.

"This . . ." Jenny stopped as she heard something else. A grating, rattling noise, almost like marbles rolling along a floor. She sat up and twisted around, just in time to see a virtual avalanche of small pebbles pouring over the edge of the rock outcropping above them. The last of the pebbles wasn't so small, though. In fact, it wasn't a pebble at all, it was more the size of a bowling bowl.

Jenny scrambled to her knees. "Sally, look out!"

Sally turned, but not fast enough. The large rock sailed through the air and hit her in the shoulder with enough force to spin her around. She grabbed her shoulder, completely off balance, one foot skidding off the edge of their breakfast spot. There was nothing to grab on to; if she fell, she'd fall ten feet before she hit more rocks below.

Jenny shot out her hand, grabbed a fistful of denim and pulled back with all her strength. Sally teetered at the edge for one more terrible second, then fell backward, her elbow jabbing Jenny painfully in the cheek as she landed half on top of her.

Sally rubbed her shoulder. Jenny rubbed her cheek. Both of them were gasping as if they'd been in a race.

"Thanks," Sally said after a moment.

"You're welcome." Jenny got to her feet and started stuffing things into the knapsack. She wanted to leave, fast.

Sally sat up, slowly. She looked shaken, but she tried for a joke. "Somebody ought to put some falling rocks signs around here."

Jenny didn't laugh. The rocks hadn't fallen, she knew that as surely as she knew her own name. When she'd looked back, before, she'd seen something besides a bunch of rocks tumbling down. She'd seen a shadow. A human shadow. The rocks hadn't fallen. They'd been pushed.

Chapter 9

Sally didn't believe her, not at first. "It was a cloud," she said as they rode the horses away from the rimrocks. She gestured over her head; the wind was skittering several puffy clouds across the sky. "They make funny shadows on the ground, you know that."

"It wasn't a cloud," Jenny said. "I know what cloud shadows are like and this wasn't one of them. And don't try to tell me it was a bear."

Sally hooted. "We're not in the complete wilderness out here, no matter what some people think. Of course it wasn't some bear."

"Right. It was some*body*." Jenny was too worried to feel relief that there were no bears around. "It was another prank, I'm sure of it."

"Come on! Pranks are harmless," Sally said. "Ugly, maybe, like that snake, but harmless."

"You're saying those rocks just fell by themselves?" Jenny asked. "Just kind of slipped over the edge without any help?"

"Well, they had to have help," Sally said. "But it didn't have to be human help." She pulled Emma up so Jenny could ride alongside. "It could have been geological. You know, something like an earthquake. A little one that nobody could feel. Or maybe there was a sonic boom that shook the rocks up. It could have been anything."

"I didn't hear any sonic boom," Jenny said. "And a 'little' earthquake wouldn't be enough to move that rock, Sally. And no matter what you say, not all pranks are harmless. What about all those deaths you read about from fraternity hazings?" She took a deep breath. "I saw a shadow — a human shadow!"

"Okay, okay! Calm down," Sally said. "Maybe you're right. Weird things do keep happening to you, so maybe somebody *is* behind it all."

"But who?!" Jenny cried. "Brad? Do you think Brad did it?"

"That's for you to find out, isn't it?"

It was a strange answer, Jenny thought. Either Sally didn't really believe her and was just humoring her, or else. . . . Jenny gave her a sidelong glance. Sally was looking ahead, smiling to herself. Did she know? Did Sally know who was behind it all?

No, it couldn't be true. Sally was a little shallow, maybe, a little uncaring, but she wasn't mean. Was she?

Suddenly, all Jenny wanted to do was get home. She pushed her horse into a faster pace and held on tight, letting the pounding gait drive all the unanswered questions from her mind for the moment.

At the turnoff to Sally's house, Jenny slid off Emma's back. "I'll see you when you get back," she said. "I hope your visit's not too awful."

"Thanks," Sally said. "And thanks for grabbing me up there. I probably would have broken some bones if I'd fallen." She waved as she rode off on the winding dirt road to her house. "I'll call you in a few days!" came floating back on the dusty air.

Jenny watched until Sally and the horses rounded a bend, then hiked up the road to her house. She let herself in, patted the dog, and went straight to the answering machine.

McPherson. The younger. "Miss Fowler," he said. "Still alone, huh? Too bad."

"How do you know I'm still alone?" Jenny said out loud, hating the crude chuckle in his voice. She stopped the machine. She remembered his eyes, riveted to her bathrobe, and shivered. How *did* he know she was alone? He couldn't, unless . . . no. No, he was just guessing. Wasn't he?

Jenny started the tape again and heard him say they could start in ten days, at eight in the morning. He didn't mention her being alone again. Maybe somebody had come in while he was talking, she thought, and he couldn't say what he really wanted to say.

No, stop it. You're acting paranoid. Jenny gave herself a shake and shut off the machine. That was the only message. Nothing from her parents. And nothing from her secret admirer. Jenny wondered if he'd decided to give up. It had been a while since his last contact; maybe he'd had second thoughts. Or maybe he felt like an idiot for making the calls and sending her flowers in the first place. She wanted to tell him to keep it up. Better yet, she wanted him to march up to her door and introduce himself.

"Oh, well. Maybe he will."

Peaches, stationed at Jenny's feet, perked her ears up and whined.

Jenny smiled at her. "Have you been lonely, Peach?"

The dog wagged her stump of a tail.

"Okay. I've got dust in my hair so I'm going to take a shower," Jenny said. "Then we'll drive into town and buy some food."

Ecstasy. *Drive* and *food* were two of Peaches' favorite words.

Jenny showered off the dust and grit, and decided to let her hair dry naturally. It would look like a gone-to-seed dandelion, but she didn't want to stay in the house. She wished she had someplace to go besides the grocery store, some friend's house where she could feel comfortable and safe. Sally was leaving, but she wouldn't do, anyway. After the way she'd acted before, Jenny wasn't sure she'd ever feel comfortable with her again. And there wasn't anybody else. The store was her only escape. Later, she'd have to stay in the house whether she liked it or not. Then she could mess with her hair if she wanted to. And she might want to. There was an entire night ahead to get through; shelving books would get boring after awhile. So, she could hang pictures, put away clothes, maybe even cut her hair if she got up the nerve. That ought to take her until at least midnight. Then a movie. Then sleep. Maybe.

Peaches was delighted to be getting out. She took off toward the car in a cross between a trot and a roll, looking like a furry, stubby-legged barrel. Jenny actually had to hoist her into the back seat.

"You're pathetic," she said affectionately.

Peaches took up her usual position, her nose poking out the partially open window, her ears blown back by the wind, as Jenny, singing along with the radio, drove them into Rimrock. As usual, the road in was deserted, so Jenny was surprised to see so few parking places once they arrived in town.

The spots in front of the grocery store were all taken, so she drove up two blocks, then around, and finally found one in front of the card shop. "Come on, Peach. We're here."

A faint snore emanated from the back seat. Peaches was asleep.

Jenny shook her head, then looked around. The car wasn't in the shade. But she wouldn't be gone long and there *was* a breeze. If she left the windows down, Peaches would be fine. Besides, she remembered that the grocery store had three round stickers on its doors. One had a cigarette, one had a pair of bare feet, the third had the silhouette of a dog.

All of them had diagonal red bars through them. Peaches couldn't go in anyway.

Jenny rolled all the windows down halfway, then slid out of the car and closed the door as quietly as possible so Peaches wouldn't wake up and whine to come with her. The dog didn't budge; maybe she'd sleep the whole time. Jenny hoped so. Peaches loved a drive, but being left in the car, even for five minutes, made her howl as if she'd been abandoned for good.

The last time Jenny had been in the grocery store, she'd been the only customer there. Today it was actually crowded. Not jammed like the supermarkets she was used to, but there were enough people in the aisles to make it tricky getting her cart around. She kept an eye out for familiar faces, then realized there wasn't anyone she really wanted to see. That was when she saw Dean.

He was walking by outside, and as he glanced in the window, Jenny waved to him. He stared at her so long, she started to think he'd forgotten who she was. Finally he raised an arm and pointed to his watch, as if he didn't have time to stop. Then he turned and left.

Jenny shrugged. She didn't want to talk to him anyway. He seemed kind of aloof. But after he'd gone, she felt more alone than ever.

Bumping her way through the aisles, she bought fruit, eggs, frozen waffles, chocolate chip ice cream, cheese and crackers, hamburger meat and rolls, sliced turkey, salad makings, and a chicken to cook for when her parents came back. Then she got in one of the two checkout lines. Then she waited.

Half an hour later, she was still waiting. It wasn't a computerized supermarket. Not only that, but the man three carts ahead of Jenny had bought enough food to last at least a month. She glanced at her cart and started to think about what to put back so she could get in the express line. Then she remembered there was no express line. She sighed, hoping Peaches wasn't howling and creating a disturbance, then she pulled a tabloid from the rack. The place wasn't so old-fashioned that it didn't have tabloids.

Halfway through a story about a woman who'd been to Mars and back, and seen Elvis en route, Jenny felt a hand on her arm, and looking up, she saw Brad.

His eyes were clear this time, she noticed, and his round face was pale. "Jenny," he said quietly, "I don't really remember too much about the other night. But I think I made a fool of myself. I'm sorry."

Jenny stared at him. He seemed to mean it, but she couldn't be sure.

"Well . . ." he turned to go.

"Wait," Jenny said. "You didn't happen to leave anything at my house, did you?"

"No." He looked confused. Either that, or he was a good actor. "At least, I don't think so."

"Okay." There was no point in going on, Jenny decided. Either he'd left the snake or he hadn't. And if he had, he wasn't going to admit it.

"Well . . . okay. Bye, Jenny." Still looking slightly baffled, Brad left the store. Jenny wasn't sorry to see him go.

Finally, her turn at the checkout came. She bagged her own groceries, which seemed to surprise the girl at the cash register, but another thirty minutes had crept by, and Jenny just knew Peaches was awake by now, putting on her abandoned-animal act.

With one bag under each arm, Jenny finally left the grocery store and hurried the two blocks back to her car, straining her ears every step of the way for the howls of a miserable dog. She didn't hear them, and when she reached the car, everything was quiet.

Relieved, Jenny set her bags down and glanced in the back window. She couldn't believe it, but Peaches was still asleep, the sun picking out the pinkish highlights in her hair. Jenny laughed and rapped loudly on the window. The window . . . it was up. All the way up. She'd left it halfway down, hadn't she?

She reached for the driver's door. Locked. And its window was up, too. All the windows were up. What was going on? She fumbled in the pocket of her shorts for the keys, unlocked the door, and pulled it open. A puff of ovenlike air enveloped her bare legs: the inside of the car was baking hot.

"Peaches, what happened, you must be . . ." Jenny stopped. The dog hadn't moved. "Oh, no!"

Jenny reached over and unlocked the back door, then slid outside and yanked it open. Peaches still hadn't moved, but as she leaned in, she saw that Peaches was breathing. Barely. "Oh, Peach!"

Heat stroke. She'd read about it, knew the dog might as well have been shut in an oven, knew she was dying. Jenny heard a horrible, rasping sound and realized it was her own ragged breathing. She reached for the dog, tears filling her eyes, and felt the hot fur in her hands. Dying. Peaches was dying. *Would* die, unless. . . .

A vet. There was a veterinarian around here someplace, but where? Where! She'd have to drive around until she spotted it. She pulled back out of the car, hitting her head so hard on the roof that everything went black for a sickening moment. Gasping in pain and terror, she stumbled toward the front seat. Have to hurry, she thought. Can't stop. Can't waste a second.

Just as she was about to slide in, Jenny spotted a woman coming down the sidewalk. "The vet's!" she shouted, her throat thick with tears. "Where is it? Where's the vet?!"

The woman must have seen the panic on Jenny's face because she didn't waste words. "Middle of the next block, the sign's out front. Dr. Jacobsen."

Faster on foot. Jenny reached into the back seat, slid her arms under Peaches and pulled her out. The dog was limp and heavy, but Jenny cradled her as close as she could, then half trotted, half shuffled her way down the sidewalk. "It's okay, you'll be okay," she crooned over and over. Hurry! She had to hurry. Oh, God, poor Peach!

The waiting room was empty, but Jenny knew someone must be around because she could hear a cat meowing pitifully and a man's voice saying something soothing. She hurried over to the desk and called out, "Please, I need help! It's an emergency!"

The cat kept yowling, but Jenny heard footsteps, and in seconds a man in a white coat, liberally sprinkled with animal hair, came into view. They ought to wear brown coats, Jenny thought wildly, the hair wouldn't show so much.

"It's my dog!" she said. "She was in the car and it was hot. . . ."

The man, Dr. Jacobsen, she figured, lifted a hinged section of the desk and stepped out. Without a word, he took Peaches from Jenny's arms and strode back into the examining room, out of sight.

Jenny's shirt was pasted to her chest and her arms were shaking. She let them hang limply at her sides until they stopped. Then she sat down in a chair and waited.

The doctor was back in half an hour. He didn't waste words either. "She'll make it," he said.

Jenny didn't know she'd been holding her breath until she let it out. She stood up. "Thank you," she said in a shaky voice.

Dr. Jacobsen was about her father's age, she thought, with graying-blond hair and bright blue eyes. He would have been handsome if he'd smiled, but he wasn't smiling. "I know you didn't mean for this to happen," he said, "but I have to tell you that it was a stupid thing to do. There's just no other word for it."

"I — "

"I know, I know, you don't want a lecture," he interrupted. "Believe me, I don't like giving one, either. But it's part of the job. You just don't leave the animal in a car on a hot day like this. That's what causes heat stroke, which is what your dog has, and which could have killed her."

Jenny shook her head. "The windows . . . I left — "

"You left them cracked," he interrupted again. "You should have put them halfway down at least. Better yet, you shouldn't have left her there at all. Don't do it again."

Jenny stopped trying to explain. What could she say? The truth would just sound like a lie, like she was trying to worm her way out of feeling guilty.

The doctor must have seen the misery in her face, because his expression changed. His eyes softened and so did his voice. "End of lecture," he said. "I'll keep her here tonight and watch her tomorrow. But you should have her back on Monday." He smiled for the first time. "She seems to be basically healthy, except for a weight problem. But we can talk about that when you pick her up."

Jenny couldn't smile back. She was afraid she'd burst into tears. The best she could manage was another thank you on her way out.

Her car was exactly as she'd left it, two doors open, grocery bags dumped beside it. The frozen waffles would probably survive; she wasn't sure about the meat. But the ice cream was now a vanilla puddle topped with melting chocolate chips. Jenny found a rag in the trunk and cleaned up the mess as well as she could, then got in the car and headed home.

The tears finally came as she left town and started down the long empty stretch of road that led to her turnoff. At first she tried to blink them back, then she gave up. There were no other cars to run into anyway. She wiped her face with one hand, steered with the other, and tried to figure out what had happened.

This was no prank, she knew that. Putting someone's pet in danger wasn't prank material. Had Brad done it? He'd been in town. But so had Dean — he didn't have anything against her, did he? Plenty of other people had been around. It didn't have to be someone she knew, doing something hateful. It could have been an accident. A good deed gone wrong. Maybe Peaches had woken up, started howling and throwing herself against the doors, and then some passerby had rolled up the windows to keep her from leaping out. It was hard to believe that whoever did it could be totally ignorant about the temperature inside a closed car, but it was possible, she guessed. She didn't want to believe that someone had done it deliberately.

For a few minutes, Jenny kept reliving the whole

thing, felt the heat wash out from the car, saw Peaches's nearly lifeless form on the backseat, remembered the awful helpless feeling as she sat in the waiting room. But finally she was able to push the images away by reminding herself that Peaches was going to be all right. That was the most important thing.

The tears had dried up, and she was feeling much calmer when the car stopped. On its own. No sputtering or coughing to let her know something was wrong, either. It just coasted a few feet in silence before finally refusing to move another inch. Jenny tried to restart it, got out and looked under the hood, checked the tires, got back in, and turned the key one more time. That's when she noticed that the gas gauge was on empty. Below empty, to be more precise.

"Oh, no." She put her head against the steering wheel, not sure whether to laugh or start crying again. It was only two-thirty in the afternoon. If the rest of the day kept up like this, it was going to be the longest twenty-four hours on record.

If she just sat here for a while, somebody would come by, wouldn't they? Of course they would. But judging from the traffic on this road, it would be two or three days at least. If she was lucky.

Feeling very tired, Jenny got out and stood beside the car. Your house isn't that far away, she told herself. Three miles? Maybe less. You can do it.

She stood another minute or two, then pocketed

the keys and started down the road. That does it for the meat, she thought, glancing back at the car. She'd have to dump it the minute she got it home. Whenever that miraculous event occurred.

For the first few minutes, Jenny kept listening hopefully for the sound of another car, but after that, she became resigned to the fact that it wasn't going to happen. She didn't know where all the Saturday shoppers lived, but it obviously wasn't out this way. Nobody seemed to live out this way except her and Sally. She brightened up at that. Sally said they were leaving later this afternoon. Maybe she was still home. She'd go there first and see if they had any gas. If they didn't, at least they could drive her back to her car after she'd called a gas station.

That thought brought a little energy back to her legs, and she picked up her pace and actually smiled. When she saw the telephone booth, the smile widened into a grin.

She must have passed it every time she'd driven into town, and she'd completely forgotten about it. But there it was, set back in a little place where the road widened for cars to pull off so their drivers could make calls. Important calls, like the one she was about to make.

Jenny dug down into the bottom of her purse, which was where all the change ended up, and fished out four quarters and three dimes. Then she forgot how tired she was and started running toward the telephone booth.

Chapter 10

When she was just a few yards from the phone booth, she heard the whine of a distant engine. She stopped in her tracks and looked back down the road, ready to wave her arms and flag the driver down. This might be the only car she'd see out here, and she wasn't about to trust her luck and let it go by. The way her luck was running, the phone would be out of order.

The whine was getting louder; Jenny stepped into the middle of the road. She'd let the driver see her from a distance and have plenty of time to slow down. She was glad she was wearing white shorts and a rainbow-striped T-shirt. She'd be hard to miss.

Finally the car came into view. No, not a car, a motorcycle. As long as it has wheels, Jenny thought. And plenty of gas. She raised her arms above her head and started waving them up and down in big arcs. The motorcycle got closer.

It was black, Jenny could see now, and its rider

had on a black helmet, a sleek, space-age type that hid his face and made him look like Darth Vader. She thought of him as a he, anyway, but she couldn't really tell. She didn't really care, either, just as long as he stopped.

A few more seconds had passed when Jenny suddenly realized that the rider had no intention of stopping. He was moving toward her very fast, the whine of the engine had become a roar, and Jenny knew there was no way he could have missed seeing her bright shirt and frantically waving arms. But the engine's roar only got louder, the driver didn't slow down, and as Jenny moved quickly toward the side of the road, she felt such a rush of anger that she wanted to scream.

She *did* scream, but not in anger. She'd just reached the safety of the roadside when she turned and saw the motorcycle coming straight at her. Her scream was one of fear, and she leaped back, bumping against a corner of the phone booth and scraping her bare arm painfully on its metal edge. The motorcycle swerved, kicked up a shower of dirt and gravel, and roared off.

It had been deliberate. There was no doubt in Jenny's mind about that. She leaned against the booth, her knees actually weak and her heart pounding so loud in her ears that at first the other noise didn't even register as anything but a noise. Then she realized what it was, that it was the high-pitched whine of the motorcycle getting louder and louder. It was coming back.

She glanced around wildly, her breath coming in short little gasps. Then she felt the warm glass of the phone booth on her back, and without even thinking about it, she got herself inside and slammed the door shut.

The whine turned into a roar again, and Jenny could see the motorcycle through the glass, heading straight for the booth. She closed her eyes and sank down to the gritty cement floor, her knees jammed up against her chest. When the roar reached its highest peak, her eyes flew open, just in time to see the motorcycle swerve again, miss the booth by inches, and tear off in the other direction.

Would he come back? How much time did she have before he did? Jenny straightened up, facing the direction he'd come from if he came, and reached into her pocket for the change she'd put there when she'd been waving her arms in the middle of the road and thinking that help was on the way. Her hand shook and all the coins spilled to the floor.

Down on her knees again, she scrabbled for the money. Then she heard the motorcycle again.

She couldn't. She couldn't stay in this glass box and wait for that maniac to bear down on her again like some giant black insect homing in on its prey. She'd get out and run into the woody field behind; he wouldn't be able to follow her in there. That's where she should have gone in the first place.

As the sound of the motorcycle grew louder, Jenny grabbed the door handle and pulled. It didn't open. She tugged again, harder, then again, almost sobbing in frustration. The door was jammed. She was trapped.

Four more times Jenny looked on in terror as the motorcycle rushed toward her. She tried not to watch, but not seeing was worse, somehow. She tried to get one of the quarters into the coin slot, but her hands were slick with sweat and shaking so badly she kept dropping the money. She finally remembered that she didn't need money to make an emergency call, but by then the driver wasn't even bothering to ride off. He just turned around a few yards from the booth, the roar of his engine making it impossible to hear anything, especially an operator who'd want to know her name and location. Finally Jenny gave up and sat on the floor, her whole body tense and shaking, as the rider played his insane game. The sun beat through the glass walls of the airless booth, making it almost unbearably hot, reminding her of Peaches trapped and helpless in the baking car.

She was still thinking of Peaches when she realized that the motorcycle hadn't come back. She lifted her head and listened. No sound, except her dry, gasping breaths. She waited a minute, and when nothing happened, when no whine broke the silence, she slowly got to her feet. She carefully slotted a quarter into the phone, and punched the number of the gas station, which was conveniently displayed on a sticker on the inside of the receiver.

Busy. Jenny sobbed again in frustration and slammed the phone down. He could still come back;

he might just be waiting, letting her think she was safe.

The sweat was pouring down her body now, and the air in the booth was so steamy it hurt to breathe. Jenny grabbed the door handle and pulled, willing it to open. Her sweaty hands slipped and she fell backward, crashing into the hot glass behind her.

Hurry. She had to hurry. She had to get out or get help. She got her coins, slotted them again, and dialed.

"Bill's Texaco."

"I . . ." Jenny swallowed. Her throat felt thick.

"Yeah?" The man sounded impatient, hurried.

Jenny's words came out in a quavering whisper. "I need help! I'm stuck!"

"Lady, speak up."

"I . . . can't!" Sobbing again, Jenny held onto the phone like a lifeline.

"I can't help you if I can't hear you, lady."

Jenny tried to stop, but her stomach muscles seemed to have taken over. In and out, again and again, dry, rasping sobs that hurt her chest and wouldn't stop. She didn't know how she could keep breathing, it was so hot. So hot!

She let the phone slide from her hands and reached for the door handle. She had to get out! Her hands slipped off the handle, and she wiped them on her shorts, then grabbed the handle again and pulled. Her head felt like it might burst from the pounding, and she heard a hoarse, rhythmic, guttural sound, like an animal grunting, and realized it was coming from her. She wiped her hands again, gripped the handle, and pulled, her voice rising in pitch with the effort until she was screaming. And then, with a hideous grating of metal, the door opened.

Jenny fell backward, banging her head on the glass, and slid to the gritty floor of the booth. Too tired to move yet, she closed her eyes and felt the cooler outside air wash over her legs.

Move. She had to move. Get up and get out. She opened her eyes and was pushing herself up when she heard a tinny, distant voice. "Lady? Hey, what's going on? You all right? Lady!"

Jenny took a deep, shaky breath, got to her knees, and reached for the dangling receiver.

It was late afternoon when Jenny finally turned the car into the driveway of her house. She shut the engine off and reached for the door handle. Peaches had been in all day, she thought, she'd need a walk. Then she remembered that Peaches wasn't home, and she sank back against the car seat, closing her eyes in exhaustion. Her head was pounding and her clothes were still damp with sweat. She needed a shower, some aspirin, something cold to drink. But for the moment, all she could do was sit.

She'd told the man from the gas station to come to the phone booth. To walk down the road to her car, risking another encounter with the madman on the motorcycle, was impossible for her, like stepping into the unknown. So she'd stayed with the known — the hot, stinking telephone booth — and waited. When the Jeep arrived, Jenny knew she'd be grateful to Bill's Texaco for the rest of her life.

The man had definite opinions about everything, all of which he shared, and none of which Jenny heard. If she told him what had happened, she was sure he'd give her his opinion about that too, but she just sat dully in his Jeep, nodding from time to time as he drove her back to her car. He'd probably tell her to call the police, and she knew she should. But later. After she got home and locked the doors. After she was safe.

Now, sitting outside in the driveway, Jenny closed her eyes. She could barely think of going into that house and being alone again. She hadn't felt safe there since they'd moved to Rimrock. And the police? What would they say when she told them what she'd decided: that what had happened with the motorcycle wasn't an isolated incident, that starting with the headless snake, someone was trying to scare her. And that someone was succeeding.

The police would want to know why, and at the moment, Jenny didn't have an answer. But it was true, she knew it. She should have known it all along.

She put her hands to her temples and rubbed, trying to ease the pounding, telling herself to get out of the car, but her body just wouldn't cooperate. She felt herself sinking into a doze and when she heard the music, she thought she must be dreaming.

She opened her eyes. The music didn't stop. It wasn't quite music, though, just a few notes, hauntingly beautiful, drifting through the air.

Jenny slid out of the car and started for the house, mystified and enchanted with the sound. When she reached the porch, she saw the wind chime. Six long metal tubes suspended from a small circle of smooth wood, moving slowly in the gentle breeze. It was hanging from the same piece of wrought iron where she'd found the basket of wildflowers, and Jenny knew exactly who'd put it there. For the first time in this endless day, she remembered that she had an admirer.

She touched the chimes, setting off another peal of notes, then unlocked the front door and went inside to see if he'd called, too. There was a message, but it was from her father: everything had been worked out; he and her mother would be arriving tomorrow at six in the evening. Maybe the next call would be from her secret admirer, and she'd be home, and the two of them would actually talk. More than anything else right now, Jenny wanted someone to talk to.

Moving like a sleepwalker, she dragged herself upstairs, peeled off her filthy clothes and stepped into the shower. She'd done this just a few hours before, she remembered, but it seemed like days. Her head was still aching when she finished, so she swallowed an aspirin. Then she put on her oldest, softest pair of jeans and a dark-green, oversized

T-shirt, wrapped her wet hair in a towel, and went back downstairs.

If Mom was here, she'd tell you to eat, Jenny thought. She went back outside to the car and got the food, threw out the chicken, the turkey, and the hamburger meat, and forced herself to eat some cheese and an apple. Part of an apple. She couldn't finish it. She was hungry, but her mind had started working again and the thoughts that whirled around inside didn't go well with food.

Nobody was playing pranks: harmless, innocent pranks. Someone wanted to scare her, to frighten her so badly that she'd . . . what? Leave town? That's what she felt like doing. If she could, she'd move away and never come back.

But why? Why would anyone want to do that to her? What had she done to make someone hate her so much? And who was that someone?

The house was too quiet. She was getting jumpy again, so she unwrapped her hair and went out on the porch. The sun was getting low, but as long as there was light, she felt safe. She sat on the steps, only three feet from the door in case she wanted to run back inside, and listened to the soothing sounds of the wind chime.

Be logical. Organize your ideas. That's what teachers were always saying, not to mention her parents. Of course they were talking about research papers, not hate-filled maniacs, but that was beside the point. Jenny combed her fingers through her wet hair and tried to get her thoughts in order.

The snake. It had started with the snake. So what had she been doing before the snake arrived? Recovering from an almost-sleepless night. Her first night alone in the house, when Peaches had heard something outside. The day before, she'd taken her parents to the airport, and then what? Then she'd heard about Diana.

The air was still warm, but Jenny shivered as she remembered. She'd gone into town, to the diner, and at first, everyone was happy, joking over their hamburgers. Jenny shivered again. Then Brad had come, and the happy crowd learned that Diana had fallen on the rimrocks. And Jenny told everyone about the shout she'd heard and the scream. And Brad had been furious because she couldn't remember the words. She still couldn't remember. Was he still so furious that he wanted to hurt her? Just because she couldn't remember? Remembering wouldn't help Diana, he had to know that.

Jenny shivered again and wrapped her arms around her knees. The awful things had started happening the day after she'd told everybody about the shout. The shout. She squeezed her eyes shut and tried to hear it again, not the words, just the sound, the feeling.

It wasn't hard to bring the feeling back to life. The wind and thunder and lightning. Her own fear, and her own shouts for David. She squeezed her eyes tighter. There'd been a big flash of lightning, and she'd screamed, then she'd heard someone shout. And then she'd heard someone scream. Someone else.

Jenny's eyes flew open, but she didn't see anything except the dark, rain-drenched rocks of the bluff. The wind chime was still making its haunting music, but she heard nothing except the shout and the scream. And the voices. Not just one. *Two* voices. She'd heard two different voices. One shouted and one screamed. Two different people. Not just Diana, alone, but two people up there. And then Diana fell. And whoever was with her knew it, and left her there, knowing she was hurt. Knowing she might die.

Jenny's heart sped up, sending a rush of blood to her face, a rush of fear. Then you came along the next day, she told herself, talking about what you'd heard. And whoever was up there with Diana was listening to every word. And got scared that you'd remember. Diana was in a coma; *she* wouldn't say anything. The only person to worry about was big-mouthed Jenny Fowler. And the thing to do was make sure she didn't remember. To play tricks on her and scare her so badly she wouldn't think of anything but what was happening to her.

Well, it had almost worked. Jenny had tried her best to forget that night on the rimrocks, anyway. She'd even tried to convince herself that there was some idiot, junior-high prankster behind all the tricks, laughing up a storm. Whoever was behind them wasn't laughing, though. He or she was deadly serious.

Suddenly Jenny jumped up, unable to sit still any longer. She was so scared she wanted to run. But where could she run to? Who could she run to? She was alone. Just like he wanted.

He? Brad? Jenny thought again of the big, good-looking football player and the desperation on his face when she couldn't remember what she'd heard. And that visit he'd made to her house, when he'd said how he hated Diana. Jenny had been scared then, scared of the fierceness in his eyes and the way they glittered whenever he looked at her. But that fear was nothing compared to what she felt now, now that she knew someone was out to get her. Someone crazy with anger, so crazy he'd pushed Diana off the rimrocks. That someone could be Brad.

Sally thought Brad had sent the snake. But Sally had been the one to deliver it. She said she'd found it on the porch, but she could have brought it. And she'd acted so strange this morning, up on the rimrocks, so nervous. Looking at her watch, like she was waiting for something to happen. Could she have arranged the fall of rocks, not knowing it would go wrong? Could she be in it with someone else? With Brad?

Jenny shook her head. It was hard to believe. But it was hard to believe that any of this was happening at all. It *was* happening, though. If she wanted to be safe, she'd better figure out who was doing it.

Jenny paced the porch, her mind racing, flitting

back and forth over the people she knew, until it finally landed on Dean. Dean Latham. In spite of that wink he'd given her, Jenny thought he was a cold fish. So calm, so rational, so logical when he'd talked about how sound could play tricks. And Jenny had agreed, thinking he was just trying to be nice. Her mind hadn't played any tricks, though, she knew that. But Dean might be. And he'd been in town today, she'd seen him. He could have shut the windows of her car. If he'd pushed Diana, or left her there, then he'd want to be very sure about what Jenny heard.

There was someone else who wanted to be sure, too, and Jenny's mind finally turned to David. She'd been putting him off, not wanting to face it, not wanting to admit that he could be the one. But he could. He'd been as anxious, as desperate as Brad for her to remember what she heard. And he'd been with her on the rimrocks. And that time they'd been separated was when he could have been with Diana, instead of looking for a bird's nest, like he said.

Jenny stood up, shaking her head. Not David, she told herself. Not him. But why not? Just because he'd kissed her? Just because she was half crazy about him twenty minutes after they first met?

What about the second time they met, when he'd come back to the diner, and the third, when he'd followed her into town? She thought he was mad at her those times, or had changed his mind about her. But now she realized there might be another reason for the way he'd acted. Pushing her to remember what she'd heard, asking her if she'd seen Diana, acting so jumpy, so secretive — he could have a secret, all right. A deadly one.

"You don't really know him," she said aloud. "You don't really know any of them."

The breeze picked up, blowing the wind chime and making its bell-like notes ring out more clearly. Jenny listened gratefully to the sound, wishing it were even louder, so loud it would drive everything else from her mind. She didn't want to be thinking these thoughts, suspecting people, feeling terrified. If she told anyone, they'd probably think she was crazy.

Half an hour before, she probably would have agreed. But not now. Not since she'd remembered that other voice, and knew that someone had been with Diana on the bluff. No one could convince her she was crazy now. But there was no one to tell, either.

Again, Jenny felt an overwhelming urge to run — anywhere — but there was nowhere to go. If only she had a friend, a safe place to go to, just for a while, until she could decide what to do. Her eyes burning, her throat dry, she stumbled into the house and gulped down two glasses of water, then bent over the sink as her stomach heaved. She didn't get sick, but she felt so lightheaded that she lurched into the living room like a cartoon-drunk and fell onto the couch.

Finally her head stopped spinning, and she sat

up and looked around. Through the windows, she could see the rimrocks blazing red from the setting sun. She turned away from them, and as she did, she saw that the answering machine's light was on. While she was out on the porch, so caught up in her horrible, logical thinking that she wouldn't have heard the ringing phone, someone had called and left a message.

She pushed herself off the couch, walked to the desk, and punched the button.

"Jenny? Did you like the music? When I saw the chime and heard the sound it made, I thought of you. I hope you like it. That's why I'm calling."

There was a pause. Jenny stared at the phone, feeling her tension start to ease. His voice was so friendly, so warm, she wished it could keep her company all night long. All night? Could she really stay in this house alone for another night, knowing what she knew?

"No." His voice was a little stronger now. "That's not why I'm calling. Not the only reason, anyway. I think . . . I know these phone calls and the presents must seem like a joke to you. I hope they don't, but I wouldn't blame you if they did. They're not a joke, Jenny, but they are getting laughable."

Another pause, and Jenny heard him take a breath. She took one, too.

"So will you meet me? It's almost six now. If you get home any time in the next hour, will you meet me? I know I should come to your house, but I have to be at my job by seven-thirty, and it's in the opposite direction, almost in Mount Harris." He took another breath and laughed softly. "Also I . . . well, you've probably figured out that I'm not Mr. Outgoing. I mean, ringing the doorbell, making conversation with your parents, I'd probably make a rotten first impression. Couldn't we just be together first, someplace quiet? After all, you might not like me. But if you do, I'll come to your house next time and make the best impression I can. Promise." A slight pause, then he went on. "There's a place I like. It's on the way to my job. You could come and we could talk. Face to face, finally."

He went on to describe the place he liked, and as she listened, Jenny realized he was talking about the rimrocks.

When he finished giving directions, he took another deep breath. "I hope you come, Jenny," he said. "I'll be waiting for you. If you can't make it, don't worry, I'll understand. But I sure hope you can."

The message was over. Before it could erase itself, Jenny pressed the save button, thinking that she'd listen to it again.

Instead, she found her purse, took out her billfold and stuffed it in the pocket of her jeans. Then she ran through the house, turned on every light, turned on the radio loud enough so anyone coming by would think there was a party in progress, and ran out the door.

She wanted someplace to run to and her admirer's message had made her think of one: the airport in Mount Harris. She'd go there and wait through tonight and tomorrow for her parents' flight to come in. Plenty of people spent the night in the airport, and if anyone asked, she'd just tell them she missed a connection.

First, though, she'd make a stop at the rimrocks. A quiet place, a quiet talk with a shy, gentle-voiced boy. Someone who cared, who she could feel safe with. A boy so gentle that he had said he would understand if she didn't meet him. That was what she needed now, someone soothing, quiet, and caring.

She wasn't even afraid of the rimrocks if her secret admirer was there.

Chapter 11

By the time Jenny turned her car onto the bumpy drive that led to the bottom of the bluff, the sun was almost down. But she knew it would be a while yet before all the light left the sky. They'd have plenty of time to sit and talk and get to know each other.

She stopped the car and got out, looking around. The rimrocks weren't so bloodred now; they'd faded to a soft, pale pink, with purplish shadows created by overhanging rocks. The breeze was still blowing, and the air smelled of pine, even though there weren't any trees around. It was nice now, she decided. A perfect setting, something she might see in a movie.

It *was* kind of like a movie, now that she thought about it. Shy boy finally gets up the courage to meet the girl he's been worshiping from afar. Picks the most romantic place he knows, a place with soft lighting and gentle breezes and . . . Jenny shook her head and smiled. She was getting carried away. First she had to meet the guy. Then she'd see if this meeting had Hollywood potential.

She was sure he'd be there already, very visible, but as she picked her way through the low bushes and scattered rocks toward the bottom of the bluff, she didn't see anyone waiting for her. He couldn't be hiding, she thought. Nobody was *that* shy. Could he have changed his mind?

She stopped walking and looked behind her. Hers was the only car there. She listened, hoping to hear another one coming, but everything was quiet. She looked toward the rimrocks again, and picked out the place he'd told her to come to. It was easy to spot, an enormous flat-topped rock right in the middle of the center section of the U-shaped bluff. It was about ten or fifteen feet up, but very easy to get to. He said she couldn't miss it, and she didn't. What she missed was someone sitting on it, waiting for her.

He'd decided not to come. No he hadn't; he'd just gotten held up or something; stop jumping to the bleakest conclusions and give him a chance, at least. Jenny argued back and forth with herself a few more times, and then finally started walking toward the rendezvous point. She couldn't believe he wouldn't show up, but even if he didn't, she felt comfortable. Which was strange, considering the way she'd always felt about the rimrocks. Maybe it was just the time of day. Or maybe she was just so tired she didn't have the energy to worry about anything. Whatever it was, she decided to climb to the rock and wait. For a while.

She reached the flat-topped rock in about fifteen minutes, using her usual climbing method of skirting every boulder in the way and walking up the gullies instead. Her stomach was back to normal and rumbling; she wished she'd eaten more than the warm cheese and apple. But maybe he'd bring a picnic. Food was always a good icebreaker.

The rock was still warm from the sun. If it had been soft, Jenny would have stretched out on it and closed her eyes. She was really tired. A single day wasn't long enough for everything that had happened. The things she'd gone through should be stretched out over a couple of weeks, at least.

But she didn't want to think about that. Later, when she wasn't so fuzzy-headed, she'd decide what to do. Right now, she just wanted to keep her mind empty and let her secret admirer fill it with whatever he wanted.

She wasn't wearing her watch. When she left the house, it had been almost six-thirty. He'd called at six. Anytime within the next hour, he'd said. The hour must be almost up. She sat cross-legged on the warm rock and looked down below. Her car was still all by itself, a dusty brown shape among the lengthening shadows.

She put her head in her hands and closed her eyes for a few seconds. It was a chancy thing to do. She'd never slept sitting up before, but the heat from the rock and the soft wind through her hair made up for the hardness of the seat. Her head dropped lower, and she brought it up with a jerk. If she sat here much longer, she'd really fall asleep and probably roll right off her perch.

She stood up and stretched. The rock was big enough for pacing, so she tried that for a while, then sat down again. The rock wasn't as warm as before. And the light was changing, too. Pretty soon she wouldn't be able to see her car. It was still peaceful, but as far as she was concerned, the peace ended when the sky got dark. If he didn't show up in a few more minutes, she was leaving.

"Jenny?"

What was he, a mind reader? She stood up again, brushing off the seat of her jeans. She hadn't seen him coming, and she had a bird's-eye view of the territory. "I'm here," she called. "Where are you?"

She heard a small sound that might have been laughter. "Up here, above you."

Jenny turned and looked, but couldn't see anything. Another rock jutted part way over the one she was on and blocked her view. She ran her fingers through her hair, wishing she'd thought to stick a comb in her pocket when she'd gone tearing out of the house.

"Don't bother with that," he called. "You look fine."

Jenny dropped her hands, feeling like she'd been caught at something. "Where'd you come from?"

"The top."

Of course, she thought, the bluff's flat on top. There's even a road up there. Maybe he lived up that way.

She started to fiddle with her hair again, then stopped. "This isn't fair," she laughed. "I can't see you. Come on down, why don't you?"

"I've got a better idea. You come up here to me," he told her. "Getting up's easier than getting down at this point."

Jenny had her doubts about that. "I'm not much of a climber," she said. "And it's getting hard to see."

"You'll do fine," he assured her. "And I'll start down, so we'll meet halfway, okay?"

It was funny, Jenny thought. She'd been shouting almost, but his voice was still the same soft, gentle one she'd heard on the phone. And it was still unrecognizable. Each time he spoke, she tried to place it, but couldn't. She wanted to see his face, so she might as well climb.

"Okay," she said. "Just tell me which way to go. All I can see from here is another rock. And it doesn't have any steps carved into it."

Another soft sound. Definitely a laugh. "Just get off the rock, the side with the gully on it," he said. "You'll be able to follow the gully for a while before you have to do any serious climbing. And by then, I'll be down to you. It's not hard, Jenny, believe me."

Jenny didn't like the sound of the words "serious climbing," but she decided to go as far as she could.

"Okay," she called. "I'm on my way."

"So am I," he called back.

Jenny scooted off the rock and into the gully, which was about six inches wide and full of pebbles. But he was right, it did go on for quite a distance. Sometimes she had to scramble over a group of big rocks, but she always found the path again. Every once in a while she called out to make sure he was still coming, and he'd call back and say yes, he was on his way.

She kept her eyes on her feet most of the time, so she didn't notice how much darker it was getting until the gully finally ended. She looked up then and found herself facing what looked like a smooth wall of stone. It seemed to go up forever. There was no way she could climb up that.

As if he'd read her mind again, he said, "It's not as bad as it looks, Jenny. Just move a few feet to your right, and you'll see a kind of gap in the rock, a split. There are plenty of footholds in there."

Jenny did as he said and found the gap. But it was shadowy. The whole place was shadowy now.

"Come on Jenny," he said. "I'm almost down to you. I'll be able to give you a hand in a minute."

At least he's right about that, Jenny thought. His voice was much closer now. She braced her hands on either side of the split in the rock, put her foot up, found a hold, and dragged the other one up beside it. The rock wasn't as straight up as it looked. It slanted just enough so that she didn't feel like a fly on a wall. Not quite, anyway. "This must be the serious climbing you were talking about," she commented.

"You're doing great," he said. "Not much farther."

One foot up, wedge it in, bring the other foot up. Good thing she was wearing jeans or she wouldn't have any skin left on her knees. Jenny was feeling almost confident when her wedged foot came unwedged and slipped out. She gasped and clung to the rock with both hands, found her foothold again, and steadied herself.

"You okay?"

"Yes." Jenny swallowed a few times. "But listen, I don't like this," she said. "I think I want to go back down. I'd feel a lot happier with something flat under my feet."

"But you're almost here."

"Almost isn't there, though. I don't like this," she said again. "Why don't I wait while you come the rest of the way down to me? Or I could go all the way down and you could go all the way up and we could meet somewhere. Like at the diner, maybe. It's got a floor."

She'd been talking in a joking way, so she wouldn't sound whiny and chicken, and she expected him to chuckle at least. But he didn't.

"Come on, Jenny. Don't quit now." His voice was still soft. Soft and encouraging.

"I'm not quitting," Jenny said, starting to feel annoyed. "I just don't like the idea of climbing around here in the dark anymore. That's not why

I came, you know. I came to meet you."

"Then do it."

"What for?" Jenny couldn't believe it; they were arguing and they hadn't even met yet. "By the time I get up there, it'll be really dark, and I won't be able to see your face anyway. I'm going down."

"No, don't! You can't stop now, Jenny!" He was yelling, his voice no longer soft and intriguing, but hoarse with desperation. "I was counting on you!"

The words bounced off the rocks, and Jenny stopped, listening as they echoed in her mind. Closing her eyes, she heard them again. But not an echo this time. A memory. A memory of a few nights before when windswept rain had battered the bluff, when lightning tore across the sky and the thunder seemed to shake the rocks. And she'd been cowering in a little ditch, shouting for David, calling over and over until she finally heard what she thought was an answering shout.

"I was counting on you!" That's what she'd heard. Words shouted in fury, in a voice that cracked with anger and fear. But not shouted to her, to Jenny. They were shouted at Diana. The very same words, shouted by the very same voice.

"You." It came out on a rush of breath; she hadn't meant to say it.

But he'd heard. "Me what? Me what, Jenny?"

"Nothing. I . . . nothing." He was the one, Jenny was thinking. He was the one with Diana that night, and he was the one who'd called Jenny all those times, pretending he cared. He'd left Diana to die and now he was after Jenny. Because she'd heard. And now she remembered.

"Oh, Jenny." He almost moaned her name. "You know, don't you? You remember."

Jenny didn't answer. She was poking her foot around, trying not to think about anything but finding the foothold below. Where was it?! "Remember what? I don't know what you mean."

"You can't run, Jenny. It's too late for that. I know this place and you don't."

Jenny heard a movement above her and knew he was coming down. She couldn't see him. She could hardly see anything. She finally got her toe into a hole and eased herself down. A cascade of pebbles bounced from above, landing on her head and shoulders. He was coming.

"If you hadn't remembered, I wouldn't have done anything," he said, and his voice was closer. "I just wanted to talk and sound you out. I heard you up here that night, but I was hoping you hadn't heard me. But you had. So I tried all those other things, the snake and the motorcycle and that fat mutt of yours, to get you so crazy and scared, you'd leave. Just pack up and take off."

The same one, Jenny thought. The shy, warm boy on the phone and the crazy guy who'd terrorized her were the same one. And she'd never guessed. She gritted her teeth; she couldn't find the next toehold. She bit her lips and felt wildly with her foot, stretching her leg as far down as it would go.

"But it didn't work," he said. "You didn't go

away. And it's really too bad, Jenny."

Jenny found the toehold. At the same time, she heard a swift, brushing sound almost on top of her. Before she had a chance to look up, she felt a strong hand on her shoulder. With one big push, her secret admirer sent her tumbling back off the face of the rimrocks.

Something kept tickling her face. Something feathery soft and maddeningly persistent. Dog whiskers, maybe. Peaches?

Jenny reached her hand up and brushed her cheek, felt the soft something drift down her neck and into her shirt, and came fully awake. To darkness.

It took only a second to remember. She wasn't in bed, with Peaches nuzzling insistently at her to wake her up and be taken out. She was somewhere on the bluff, and part of its gritty dust was still sifting down her face.

She brushed off as much as she could, then closed her eyes again, taking stock. She was almost in a sitting position, her back up against a very hard rock. There was a sore, burning feeling along her backbone and throbbing on the side of her head. Her palms stung and one elbow ached, but the ache didn't get any worse when she moved it. She must have twisted somehow on the way down, bracing herself with her feet and hands and scraping her back along the rocks as she fell.

Fell. That was hardly the right word for it. She

opened her eyes and sat up straighter, her heart beating faster as she remembered that awful moment when she felt his hand push against her shoulder. Her secret admirer's hand. The one person she thought she didn't have to fear.

She'd been so stupid! Where was her mind? She let herself be seduced by a soft voice and actually followed it up here! Followed it just minutes after she'd told herself that she couldn't trust anyone, not even Sally.

Well, she was pretty sure Sally was out of the picture. But her "admirer's" identity was still a secret. Sure, she'd heard his voice, but that didn't mean a thing. He'd probably disguised it, given it a different pitch or something. There must be patterns in his speech he couldn't disguise; someone who knew him well probably wouldn't be fooled. But, as she'd told herself not too long ago, she didn't know anyone here that well. Not even David.

Jenny shifted around, but the rocks and sand underneath her started slipping, and she did, too. It was so dark, there wasn't even a moon. What if she slipped some more, right into the air?

If her mouth and throat hadn't been so dry and full of grit, she might have screamed. She felt like it, felt like screaming and screaming until somebody heard and came to help.

She shifted again, carefully, and heard rocks clattering down. They seemed incredibly loud, probably because everything else was so quiet. The only other sound she could hear was her own breathing.

It wasn't steady, but at least she was doing it. At least she was alive.

Did he know she was alive? He must have checked after he pushed her, Jenny thought. He must have come down and checked. But if he'd done that, then he would have known she wasn't dead.

Did he think she was in a coma, like Diana? No, he couldn't have taken a chance on that. If he'd seen she was still alive, he would have killed her.

He couldn't have seen, then. He didn't know for sure. He must not have been able to get to her. He must be waiting. Waiting until there was just enough light to see by. Then he'd make his move.

Jenny put her hands over her mouth and gulped down the sound that was trying to escape. She had to be quiet. But she also had to move, get down, get away. She didn't know what time it was, it could be hours before the first light, or it could be minutes. She had to move now. And she had to do it without him hearing her.

Chapter 12

In spite of the urge to start scrambling down immediately, Jenny forced herself to sit still for a few more minutes. The darkness was almost total; her eyes had adjusted enough so that she could make out shapes close by, but when she tried to see for any distance, it was as if a thick black cloak had been thrown over the world. It must be cloudy, she thought. She couldn't even see any stars above her, just more darkness.

She stretched her arms out wide, trying to get a feel of the place where she'd landed, and whether or not there were any sheer drops in store for her when she made her first move. Her hands met with rocks, and after she'd pulled on one to make sure it wasn't going to come loose and fall with her, she held on tight and started to roll over onto her knees. That's when she felt the pain in her right ankle. The sharpness of it made her hiss through her teeth and sweat broke out on her forehead. When the pain eased into a dull ache, she reached down and felt her ankle, gently.

It felt puffy. Did broken bones swell? She didn't know. Probably it was sprained; she must have twisted it when she landed. She couldn't let it hold her back, though, broken or not. She might have to move even more slowly than she'd planned, but she still had to move.

She grabbed hold of the rock again and rolled over. She poked around with her good foot until she felt it come up against something solid, then took a deep breath and slowly let herself slide down.

She had no idea how high she'd climbed before he'd pushed her, but she kept hoping to find that gap in the rock. After a few minutes, though, during which she covered about two feet, she knew she wasn't going to. She thought she'd fallen straight backwards, but when she twisted, she must have twisted in the opposite direction from the way she'd come. Her foot never slid into any familiar holes, and she had no other landmarks to go by. If she could just see, she'd probably see that the gap was only a few feet to one side or the other. But there was no way of telling in the darkness, and she wasn't about to start scrambling around searching for it. Her ankle wouldn't cooperate, and even if it weren't hurt, she was no fleet-footed mountain goat. She grabbed hold of another well-planted rock and slid backwards and down another few inches.

Every move Jenny made created a small landslide of rocks and gravel. Their skittering noise drove her crazy. If she could hear it, so could he. She'd move, wait for the noise to stop, try to hold her breath, and listen for some other sound. She never heard one, but that didn't mean anything. He was there, she knew it. He was waiting, probably hearing every move she made. He had to hear her, she was clattering around like a one-woman band.

So what was he waiting for? Why didn't he come and get it over with? Was he just hoping she'd fall? Or was he standing there at the bottom, listening to her trying to be quiet, waiting until she got down to him?

If that was it, Jenny knew she didn't have much of a chance. She couldn't run, not on her bad ankle. She stopped and rested, breathing in rock dust, trying to figure out what to do. She couldn't go up. But she couldn't stay put, either. Even if he was down there, she had to keep going. She couldn't outwait him; she'd go crazy if she stayed still.

It seemed endless. Between the sliding and the resting, the groping around for something solid to hang on to, and the waiting for the pain in her ankle to ease, Jenny figured a snail could have outraced her. It was impossible to go straight down; three or four times her foot had hit nothing but air, and she had to heave herself sideways until she found a safer route. But with all the slipping and scrabbling, she never came across that gap in the rock. She had no idea where she was. Down was the only direction she was certain about.

It was during one of her rest-stops that she felt

something had changed. Not the rocks, they were just as hard as ever. Not her ankle, it was still on a regular cycle of sharp pain and dull ache. But something was different. She tilted her head back, tired of inhaling dust, and that's when she figured it out: the sky had changed. It was still dark, but not the pitch-black darkness of before. Here and there her eyes were able to pick out a difference in shading, and she knew she was seeing the clouds. Morning was coming, and the sky was going to get lighter. It would be gradual, but it wouldn't be long before the light would be bright enough for Jenny to see by. And to be seen by.

She had to try to move faster now. She'd started out hating the dark, but after a while she realized it was about the only thing going for her. It was like a cover, and once morning came, that cover would be ripped off. She wouldn't be able to sneak back to her car then, or find some crevice to crawl into and hide. There hadn't been much chance of that to begin with, but once the light came, the chance would be completely gone. He'd see her, no matter where she was.

Moving faster was something she could only do in her mind, though. Her heart raced, but the rest of her just plodded along at the same agonizing slow pace. She was afraid to look up again, afraid to see even more light; she focused her eyes on the rocks about two inches from her nose and tried to forget everything else.

After a few more minutes, Jenny's foot hit air

again. She reached out with her left arm and felt a smooth, flat surface. She couldn't tell how far it went on, but to the right there was just more air, so she stuck out her left foot and managed to slide a few feet until she felt solid rock underneath. She felt to the left again. More flat rock. And more. Maybe it was the rock where she'd first come to meet him. If it was, then the gully was over to her left. And once she got to that, she could stand up and walk the rest of the way down. No, she couldn't do that, not on her ankle. She'd have to crawl. But that wasn't so bad; she should keep low, anyway.

It was still quite dark, and as she turned over on her seat and started scooting to the other side of the rock, Jenny felt a surge of hope. She was certain he was waiting for her, but if she'd actually made it down off the face of the cliff before the first light, then she might have a chance after all.

She scooted a few feet, then stopped. Her ankle was killing her and her good leg was cramping from holding all her weight. She stretched it out and rubbed it frantically. She couldn't stop now.

There. It was okay. She got ready to move, braced herself on her hands, and pushed up on her good leg. And stopped in that position, not moving, not even breathing.

She'd heard something. A sound, but not one she'd made. Silently, she eased herself down and listened.

There it was again. A rock clattering on another

one, followed by a soft swish of smaller pebbles. She knew that sound, all right, she'd been making it all night. But she hadn't made this one. Someone else had.

Automatically, Jenny reached around until her fingers closed over a loose rock. It was perfect, rough and uneven, just the right size for her hand. Then she waited again.

She heard another clattering, and then a voice, calling her name. "Jenny? Jenny!"

She bent her head, and for a second, her eyes filled with tears. He hadn't bothered to disguise his voice this time. Why should he? It didn't matter anymore, not to him. But it mattered to her. The voice she'd heard belonged to David.

"Jenny?"

She remained perfectly still, listening. She was now dry-eyed and thinking hard. He was over to her left somewhere, not to the right where the gully was. More than anything, she wanted to keep moving to the right. But she knew she had to go left, and wait for him to get her near her. Near enough so she could use the rock.

"Jenny!" He wasn't shouting, but there was fear in his voice.

Good, she thought. Maybe he thinks he's lost you. So let *him* be scared. Let him be the one who's afraid.

Quietly, she began moving toward the sound of his voice. When she reached the edge of the flat rock, she scooted back as far as she could go, got on her knees, braced herself with her good foot, and waited.

It didn't take long. She heard the shifting of gravel again, and then she could hear his breathing. It was lighter now, and she saw him move. He was climbing toward her.

"Jenny? Are you up here? If you can, answer me!"

When his head was almost level with hers, Jenny gave her answer. Her arm was already back, and with every bit of strength she had, she brought the rock crashing down on his head. She cried out at the sickening thud, but David didn't make a sound. He fell where he was, a trickle of blood already seeping down his forehead.

She didn't know when she'd started crying, but her face was wet with tears and her hand shook as she wiped them away. She rolled to her side, away from the sight of David, and lay there, wishing she could be magically transported a million miles from there to a soft bed with clean sheets. She'd made it, she was safe, but she was suddenly so exhausted she wasn't sure she could move another inch.

She had to, though. Had to get all the way down and hobble to her car, drive to the police. She forced her eyes open, and for the first time was able to pick out actual shapes. She *was* on the rock she'd first climbed to. The light was coming fast now; if she sat up, she might even be able to see her car.

Keeping her face turned away from David, Jenny

pushed herself up and looked out below. There was her car, barely visible. The sight of its shadowy bulk cheered her up, and she smiled. She could make it.

"There you are."

Nothing could have startled her more; Jenny yelled at the sound of the voice and looked around wildly. David?

"Over here, Jenny."

It was Dean Latham. Standing in the gully on the other side of the rock, his calm, pale eyes gazing at her steadily.

"What . . ." Jenny's voice cracked. She tried to clear her throat. "What are you doing here?"

"Looking for you."

"But . . ." she had to swallow again. "Why? I mean, what . . ." Jenny shook her head. Had she left her mind somewhere up on the bluff? She couldn't hold onto a single thought long enough to get it out.

"Don't bother talking," Dean told her. "It's probably better if you don't say anything."

"I have to talk," Jenny managed to blurt out. "You don't know . . . or do you? You must. Why else would you be up here looking for me?"

"I don't know what?"

"What's been happening!" Jenny flung her hand out, gesturing at David. She was still clutching the rock she'd hit him with, and she held onto it, turning it over and over in her hands as she tried to put a coherent sentence together. "He was after me. He tried to kill me. And he would have if I . . ."

"If you hadn't bashed him in the head?" Dean smiled at her and his voice was cool. "Poor David."

"Poor . . . ?" Jenny couldn't help feeling outraged. His sympathy was definitely in the wrong place. She was the one who'd just gone through hell. And what about Diana?

Dean had moved up onto the rock and was standing there, still watching her. Jenny frowned at him. He was awfully calm for somebody who'd just found out that one of his friends was an almost-murderer. Of course, he might be in shock. But he didn't look shocked. In fact, he looked satisfied, even pleased. Pleased with himself, as if he'd just solved a tricky problem.

She frowned at him again. She hadn't noticed it before, but now Jenny saw that Dean was dressed in black. Black jeans, black sneakers, a black, long-sleeved pullover. The only light spots were his hair and face. And his hands, clenched into fists.

Jenny's head was clearer now, and as she stared at Dean, her mind filled with questions. "I don't understand," she said.

"Understand what?"

"Why you were looking for me. And how you knew where to look." She gestured toward David. "Why you're not more upset about him, why you don't seem the least bit worried, or relieved, or whatever you should be feeling now that it's — "

"Now that it's over?" He smiled again. He said, "But it's not over, Jenny. Not yet. Haven't you figured that out?" His voice had changed while he talked, back to the one Jenny had heard when she'd come running to meet him, and earlier, on the answering machine. Back to the soft voice of her secret admirer.

Now it made sense. The black clothes, the sudden, unexplained appearance, the cool comment about David. It was Dean who'd called her up here, Dean who'd pushed her, who'd waited until daybreak to find her again. Jenny's eyes widened as she realized the danger she was in.

"I see you've figured it out now," Dean said. "I probably shouldn't have waited until you did. It would have been easier on you. But I guess I just wanted to see it through."

While he spoke, Jenny slowly got to her feet. She staggered, trying not to put any weight on her ankle, then got her balance. Dean watched her, the thin, polite smile never changing.

"In case you're wondering," he said, "I didn't push Diana. She fell by accident. It worked out very conveniently for me, though. Until you started talking about what you heard that night."

Jenny tried not to listen. Soft as it was, his voice was distracting. It kept her from thinking, and she had to think.

"Poor David," he said again. "I really do feel sorry for him. He didn't know what he was getting into."

Jenny didn't take her eyes off him. She had to be ready.

"But actually, he makes it easier for me," Dean

went on. "Everybody knew you two had hit it off. At first. And then plenty of us heard you screaming at him in town." He took a step toward Jenny. "They'll probably decide it was some kind of lover's quarrel. The two of you met and argued. The argument got physical." He moved toward her again, unclenching his hands. "They'll decide it was an accident, too. A tragic accident." He laughed, almost soundlessly. "Three accidents in a week. It's going to give this place a bad name. Everybody'll shake their heads and say they always knew how dangerous the rimrocks were. And for a while, nobody will climb up here. But then everything will get back to normal. People will forget. They always do."

Come on, come on! Jenny thought. Just a little closer.

Dean looked at her and sighed, as if she were a bothersome child who wouldn't leave him alone. He took another step. Then, finally, he glanced away from her, up to the sky, checking the light.

"Well, Jenny."

He started to say something more, but Jenny didn't give him a chance. She drew her arm back, pushed off with her good foot, and lunged at him, swinging the rock down toward his head.

Dean reached up to block her arm, his ice-blue eyes not calm any longer, but wide with surprise. Jenny tried to spin away from his grasping hand, but her ankle wouldn't support her and she fell, landing hard on her knee. She pushed with her hands, trying to get up fast, ready to fight.

But the fight was already over. Dean's balance had been off to begin with, and he never got it back. As Jenny was scrambling to her feet, she heard a small, sharp gasp. That tiny intake of breath was the only sound Dean made as he fell backward toward the rocks below.

Chapter 13

Jenny kept expecting to get hysterical. Or cry, at least. After all, it was over. She'd spent an endless night doing things the wishy-washy Jenny Fowler of a few days ago could never have done. Wasn't reaction supposed to set in now? She might even have killed someone. Shouldn't she feel something besides this strange calm that left her mind blank?

Almost blank. As she stood there, breathing deeply, the first image that came to mind was a tall glass of ice-cold water. Maybe that was hysteria, she thought.

Her eyes felt rusty from sand and lack of sleep. She blinked them, then started to rub them, and realized she was still gripping the rock. She looked at it for a moment and was still looking at it, still not really thinking about anything, when she heard a low groan off to the side.

David was struggling to his feet, and Jenny dropped the rock and limped toward him. She felt so much relief that her eyes finally filled, and she knew her emotions were waking up.

"You're all right," she said. "I'm so glad you're all right."

"Uh-huh." He touched his head gingerly, wincing as he felt the bump on it.

Jenny winced, too, in sympathy. "I'm sorry," she said. "I thought you . . . I didn't know."

But he was already up on the rock with her, his arms around her. She felt him take a deep, shaky breath and let it out, and she knew his emotions were working, too.

They stood together for a minute, not saying anything, and then Jenny pulled away and pointed. "Dean's down there," she said. "He fell. I don't know if he's dead or not." She swallowed hard and felt her knees start to shake. Now reaction was setting in.

A look of amazement in his eyes, David went to the edge of the rock and peered over. After a minute, he said, "He's alive. I can see him moving a little. I don't think he's fully awake, though."

"We have to call an ambulance," Jenny said.

David nodded. "I used my dad's car." He smiled faintly. "I'd have found you faster if I'd had a flashlight. There *is* a C.B. in the car, though. I'll use it to get an ambulance here." He helped her sit down. "I'll be back for you in a few minutes."

Jenny scooted herself to the edge of the rock and watched him run, leaping over rocks and bushes, all the way to his car. She hadn't seen it earlier; it was parked on the other side of hers. He wasn't in it long. Soon, he was hurrying back, carrying something floppy, probably a blanket. She saw him go to Dean and kneel beside him, and then she turned her eyes away.

The clouds were starting to break up, and a big section of the rimrocks was turning rosy. It was going to be a sunny day, she thought. Her parents would have good flying weather. She thought about going to bed and setting her alarm in time to meet them, then decided she'd better not. Once her head hit a pillow, she was going to sleep for a long, long time. A brass band outside her window might wake her, but an alarm clock didn't stand a chance.

She could hear David's voice. Dean must be awake, she thought. But she still didn't look at them. She didn't want to see Dean. She knew he needed help, psychiatric help, and she hoped he'd get it, even though she hadn't recovered enough to feel sorry for him yet. She was angry, but not so angry that she was afraid she might hit him or yell at him. She simply didn't want to see him, ever again.

In a few minutes, she heard David coming back. She looked up and saw that his face was working, as if he were trying not to cry. He and Dean were friends, she remembered. Maybe not close ones, but they'd known each other a long time. She didn't blame David for being upset. It was the kind of reaction she'd expected from Dean, earlier. To find out that someone you'd known and gone to school with for years was a completely different person than you thought — it was going to hit everybody hard.

David's face was calm by the time he reached her.

"Is he . . . how is he?" Jenny asked.

"I'm not sure. I think just his leg's broken, but I was afraid to move him," David said. "I told him what happened and that there'd be an ambulance soon."

Jenny was still shaking. David came and sat beside her, putting a washed-out denim jacket around her shoulders. They looked at each other and then they both spoke at the same time.

"What happened?"

"You first," David said.

She spoke carefully, trying not to leave anything out. She told him about the scary things that had happened — the snake and Peaches and the motorcycle — and how she'd finally figured out that they were because of what she'd heard up here that night. She told him about the admiring phone calls and the presents, and how happy they'd made her. How glad she was when she got the one last night.

"I felt so alone," she said. "I didn't trust anybody, obviously." She looked at the wound on his forehead, and he smiled. "I guess I was so scared and confused that I wasn't thinking straight. If I had been, I never would have come up here. It just never entered my mind that one person was doing both things."

"It probably wouldn't have entered anybody's

mind," David said. "Not anybody normal, anyway."

"Maybe. And then his voice!" Jenny went on. "I've heard Dean talk before, not much, but enough. He changed it some way, though. I just didn't recognize it. And I didn't think he was my secret admirer because of the way he winked at me that time."

"What time?"

"In the diner, just after everybody had heard about Diana," Jenny said. "My secret admirer was bashful, and anybody who winks like that isn't bashful."

"Dean's not bashful," David said. "He's always been kind of standoffish, though. Cold, I guess I'd say now. But he's not a winker, either. It must have been part of his plan. To fool you."

"Well, it worked," Jenny said. She shuddered and David put his arm around her shoulders.

They sat quietly for a minute, and then they heard the siren in the distance. "I know you're wiped out," David said, "but we've got to go. Can you make it?"

Jenny nodded and shrugged her arms into the jacket. He helped her up and across the rock. Then he lifted her down into the gully. He grabbed her around the waist, she draped an arm around his neck, and then he walked and she hopped away from the rimrocks.

It was slow going. They were only halfway to the cars when the ambulance pulled up. David helped her sit and went to join the men who came running toward them.

Jenny closed her eyes, her mind blank, while the medical crew took care of Dean. She didn't want to see him being carried away, and she only opened them again when she heard the siren start up. By then, David was beside her, helping her up.

"I said you just twisted your ankle and didn't need to ride in an ambulance," he told her. "I hope I was right. I just didn't think you'd . . ." his voice trailed off and he gestured at the white van that was speeding away.

Jenny hadn't even considered the possibility that she might ride to the hospital with Dean. The idea was so horrifying, it was almost funny, like black comedy, and she found herself laughing a little. "Thanks," she said. "I hadn't thought of that."

They went a little farther toward the cars, and when they stopped a second to catch their breath, Jenny remembered something.

"You said you told Dean what happened," she said. "Now tell me."

"That's right, I never got my turn, did I?"

"No. So tell me," Jenny said. "How did you know where to come looking for me? And *why* were you looking for me? And why didn't you seem surprised when I was telling you about Dean?" She'd just thought of that. Her mind really was not working well at all.

"You left out the fight we had the other day,"

David reminded her. "Don't you want to know why I've been acting so weird?"

"I want to know everything," Jenny said. "I've been in the dark long enough, excuse the pun."

"Okay." David took a deep breath. "First things first. Diana woke up."

"She did?" Jenny felt genuinely glad for the girl. "That's great, David. And she's going to be all right?"

"She's all right already," he said. "Anyway, she told about what happened to her. How she and Dean were arguing and she fell."

"He told me that, that it was an accident," Jenny said. "I didn't believe him."

"I guess he's not a total liar," David said, and his face looked sad for a moment. "He didn't push her, but he left her there. Just walked off and left her. Diana doesn't know that yet."

He was quiet for a moment as they started hobbling along. Then he said, "Dean's a computer freak."

"Yes, Sally told me."

"Well, he's a really bright guy and his family's the kind that pushes, you know? Gotta be the best, gotta get the best grades, get into the best college."

"Wasn't he?" Jenny asked. "The best, I mean?"

"According to Diana, his grades were dropping. I don't know why, maybe he just got tired of it. Anyway, it looked like he might not get into Harvard or Stanford or wherever. But he's not just your average computer nut, he's a brilliant one and he figured out how to tap into the school's system."

"I get it," Jenny said. "Instant A's."

David nodded. "Diana found out, and he begged her not to tell, she said. She felt sorry for him at first, and said she wouldn't. But then the school got wind of something funny going on and they started asking questions. Diana works in the office and she knew it wouldn't be long before they found out about him. Maybe about her, too."

"So she decided to tell?"

"Yes, but first she just wanted to lay it out to him, maybe convince him to confess," David said. "And he freaked. Just went crazy, yelling that he'd be ruined, that he'd been counting on her."

I was counting on you. Jenny didn't think she'd ever forget the words.

They reached the cars, and David helped her into his, saying he'd come back for hers as soon as he could.

"I have to pick my parents up at the airport later," Jenny said. "At six. They'll be expecting me."

"You'll be there," he told her. "I'll drive you."

Jenny leaned back in the seat and smiled. "At last," she said, "something besides rocks to sit on. This is dangerous, though. I may never get up."

"If you really want to walk, hop, I mean. . . ."

"Forget it," she said. "Just tell me now, about why you, all of a sudden, got so . . . I don't know, so distant. You acted like you hated me after what happened to Diana. And then you started bugging me to remember what I heard. What was going on?"

David put the key in, but didn't turn it. His dark eyes looked confused, as if he wasn't sure himself what had been going on. "That night at the scavenger hunt, remember? I gave Diana a lift. She was really upset, told me she was worried about something. She wouldn't tell me what, just said she had to work it out and it wasn't going to be easy. Then she went off with Dean. And after that, I didn't know what happened."

He shook his head, and a look of shame came into his eyes. "This is hard to say, Jenny, but I might as well be honest. There were a couple of times there when I thought it might be you." He swallowed, and then went on in a rush. "She isn't exactly the nicest person in the world, and she'd been pretty nasty to you when you met. I thought maybe after I left you on the bluff that you started climbing up, and ran into her and argued, or something. I knew you wouldn't have pushed her, but I thought . . ."

" . . . it might have been an accident?" Jenny finished.

He nodded. "Everything kept pointing to Dean, though," he went on quickly. "And I didn't want to believe it." He pounded softly on the steering wheel. "I mean, he's a friend, was a friend, I don't know. Anyway, it's not every day you suspect a friend of leaving someone to die. It made me a little crazy. I guess it was easier to think it might be you. I don't expect you to understand, but I kept telling myself I didn't really know you."

"I did, too," Jenny told him. "When I finally realized somebody was trying to scare me, I suspected everyone, even Sally. Even you," she added, glancing at his forehead. "How could I not understand why you thought those things about me, David?" she said. "I didn't trust you, either. And it's true, we *don't* know each other."

"No. I guess not," he said. They were both quiet for a minute. Then David went on, "So, anyway, there I was, thinking rotten thoughts and feeling rotten for thinking them. Then when Diana woke up and told us about Dean, I felt even worse. I came over to your house to tell you about her, but mostly I just wanted to apologize and to talk."

"But I wasn't there," Jenny said. "Why did you come looking for me here? Why were you even worried?"

David leaned his head back and grinned. "I broke into your house."

"You what? You didn't."

"Right, I didn't. You forgot to lock the door," he said.

"And you just walked right in? Not that I'm complaining," Jenny said quickly, "but what made you do that?"

"Because the place was lit up like the Fourth of July, and it sounded like a party was going on," he explained. "But I knew your parents were out of town, and nobody answered the door. So I decided to investigate."

"It's a good thing my dog wasn't there."

"Why, would it have bitten me?"

"No." Jenny giggled. "She probably would have fainted from fear. At least I know she's safe and well at the vet's." She suddenly thought of something. "You didn't go into my room, I hope. It's a mess. Don't tell me you went into my room."

"No, I didn't go into your room. What are you worrying about your room for?" He was laughing. "I went into your *living* room, so relax. It was very neat. I noticed there was a message on your machine and I thought maybe it would give me a hint about where you were."

"And it did, and you rushed over here," Jenny said. Then she thought of something else. "Wait a minute. You went to my house last night. You didn't get here until sunrise practically. I don't mean to sound picky, but . . ."

"What took me so long?" he finished. "I didn't know who'd called you. I thought you had a boyfriend."

"I just moved here, how could I have a boyfriend already?"

He looked at her, his eyes gleaming. "It's been known to happen."

"Yes. I guess it has." Jenny was suddenly very conscious of the way she must look. Her jeans were ripped, her ankle was the size of a small cantaloupe, every piece of exposed skin was scratched, and she didn't even want to think about her hair. She must be getting back to normal, she thought, if she was worrying about her hair.

David grinned at her again, as if he knew exactly what she was worrying about. "Anyway, I went home," he said. "Everybody was on the phone that night, talking about Diana and Dean. Brad called, Karen called; if Sally'd been here, she would have talked nonstop. I don't know why, but I decided to call Dean. I didn't know if he knew. That Diana had come out of the coma, I mean. I thought somebody ought to tell him and give him a chance to go to her. Apologize, maybe." He laughed softly, almost sadly.

"And he wasn't there."

David nodded. "Nobody knew where he was. That's when I figured out that he was the one you'd gone to meet. I got here as fast as I could."

That was it. There wasn't anything more to tell. David started the car, but before he drove away, he reached over and took her hand. "I should have talked to you before," he said. "If I'd told you what was on my mind, I might have saved you a lot of . . ." he sighed " . . . *trouble* is not the right word, but you know what I mean."

"Yes." Jenny held tight to his hand. "But I understand why you didn't. Don't start thinking 'What if.' I'm not going to. It's over. Let's just go on from here."

"Deal," he said. "On one condition" — he leaned across and brushed some dust from her face, then kissed her softly on the forehead — "We both said we didn't really know each other. Let's get to know each other better, okay?"

"Deal," Jenny said.

David put the car into gear and pulled away. As they drove, Jenny looked back toward the rimrocks. The sun had climbed higher; the rocks were losing their vivid rose color and fading back to sandy pink.

They still loomed, Jenny thought. But they hadn't been the cause of her nightmare. The nightmare was over, and she knew without a doubt that the rimrocks would never disturb her sleep again.

About the Author

Carol Ellis has written more than fifteen books for young people, including several for Scholastic's *Cheerleaders* and *The Girls of Canby Hall* series. She lives in New York with her husband and son.

point

SCIENCE FICTION

Enter an exciting world
of extraterrestrials and
the supernatural. Here
are thrilling stories that
will boggle the mind
and defy logic!

Point Science Fiction